D0771353

Books by
SUZANNE MARIE PHILLIPS

Chloe Doe

Burn

Lindsey Lost

LINDSEY LOST

SUZANNE MARIE PHILLIPS

viking

an imprint of penguin group (usa) inc.

VIKING

Published by the Penguin Group

Penguin Group (USA) Inc., 345 Hudson Street, New York, New York 10014, U.S.A.

Penguin Group (Canada), 90 Eglinton Avenue East, Suite 700, Toronto, Ontario, Canada M4P 2Y3
(a division of Pearson Penguin Canada Inc.)

Penguin Books Ltd, 80 Strand, London WC2R 0RL, England

Penguin Ireland, 25 St Stephen's Green, Dublin 2, Ireland (a division of Penguin Books Ltd)

Penguin Group (Australia), 250 Camberwell Road, Camberwell, Victoria 3124, Australia
(a division of Pearson Australia Group Pty Ltd)

Penguin Books India Pvt Ltd, 11 Community Centre, Panchsheel Park, New Delhi – 110 017, India

Penguin Group (NZ), 67 Apollo Drive, Rosedale, Auckland 0632, New Zealand
(a division of Pearson New Zealand Ltd.)

Penguin Books (South Africa) (Pty) Ltd, 24 Sturdee Avenue, Rosebank,
Johannesburg 2196, South Africa

Penguin Books Ltd, Registered Offices: 80 Strand, London WC2R 0RL, England

First published in the United States of America by Viking,
an imprint of Penguin Group (USA) Inc., 2012

10 9 8 7 6 5 4 3 2 1

Copyright © Suzanne Marie Phillips, 2012
All rights reserved

LIBRARY OF CONGRESS CATALOGING-IN-PUBLICATION DATA IS AVAILABLE
ISBN 978-0-670-78460-8

Printed in the USA   Set in Rotis Serif Std   Book design by Kate Renner

PEARSON

I have been blessed with amazing editors through-out my career, and for this I am so grateful. I was in a free fall when Sharyn November caught me, and it's been a soft landing. Thanks, Sharyn, for making room for me at your house.

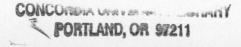

TUESDAY, JANUARY 11, 2011

I

7:15 A.M.

Micah pulls his sweatshirt over his head, stuffs his feet into his Nike trail runners—there was more snow last night—and leaves his bedroom.

Vivian had called him when the first flurries began, and they met in the field behind Bryce's Farm, where it should have been pitch-dark, but the flakes were iridescent, fluttering and sparkling as they fell. He watched while she twirled and caught them on her tongue and listed all of the things that *could* be snow, if they stretched their minds enough: rice, "the way the pods burst open in July and the wind picks them up and turns them into wishes"; white chocolate chips and cracked eggshells and whitecaps, which were "already fluffy and melt in your hand."

Micah fell into a trance listening to her. Vivian is like that. Deep. She *flows*. And sometimes he gets caught in her current and it's a free fall.

The bathroom door opens and his sister, Lindsey, steps out. Staggers out, really. Her long blonde hair is tangled, and she's bundled in sweats and furry slippers.

"Are you sick or something?" he asks.

She stops and looks at him. He hurt her feelings. He can

tell, the way her eyes get soft and fluid. It's been too easy to do that lately. Usually, Lindsey is full of comeback.

"Thanks," she says. "You sweet-talk Vivian like that?" She pushes past him. "Of course not," she says. "Because Vivian's definitely present tense, right?"

She slams her bedroom door hard enough that the walls shake.

Geez. Last night he asked her if she was okay, because her attention was drifting a lot and he had to call her name a couple of times to reach her, and she started crying. She denied it and hid her face inside her calculus book, but Micah heard the wet sniffles.

He walks to her bedroom door and taps.

She doesn't answer.

"Linds?" Nothing. He can hear her shifting through the clothes in her closet, the hangers scraping against the metal pole.

"Lindsey Michelle Hamilton," he tries, putting some of their mother into his voice.

It works. His sister opens the door and rests her face against it while gazing at him. Lindsey is older by one year, and tall, so they're eye to eye. She smiles and says, "That was funny."

"I'm a comedian," Micah agrees, but this close, the dark smudges under her eyes are almost as deep as the grease he spreads under his before a game. The rest of her face is a complete wash. "Sorry about that," he says, even though he's thinking she's got to be sick.

Of course, something as little as a cold or flu doesn't put Lindsey down. She's a high-performing athlete in her senior year of high school. She's on the fast track to a Pac-12 university. She has to go to school, has to make the grades, has to make the time on the track and put the time in at the gym, and one day the gold will be hers. That's her dream. Micah thinks it will happen. So does everyone else in their small town. And everyone in the whole state of Oregon, it seems. Lindsey placed at Nationals last year with a clocked mile that put fire under the heels of the reigning world champ.

"You look great," he tries.

"No, I don't. I didn't sleep much last night," she admits. "Or the night before that."

"What's up?"

She opens the door a little more and leans against the frame. For a minute she looks like she's going to spill it all, which is something they do a lot. But then she looks away and lifts her shoulders in a shrug. *"Pressure,"* she says, imitating Billy Joel. Sometimes, when they're both feeling it, they put that CD in and kick back on the floor in the den and sing like they're two of the Three Tenors. And when they're done they roll around, cracking up, and the pressure is gone. That easy.

Their seasons overlap. Micah has a rocket for an arm. He's got a nickname—the Comet. He throws a fastball in excess of ninety miles per hour. That's big-league.

"It's January," he points out. Lindsey's off-season.

"It doesn't stop for me," she says. "Not anymore."

Not since last summer and Nationals.

"You can slow down a little." But even as he says it, an image of their father pops into his head: the dinner table last week, the topic, perseverance. "You have to change it up," their father had told Lindsey. "Add a few more sprints to your routine. Fit another distance run into your week." Where his sister is concerned, they talk in terms of shaving seconds and milliseconds off her time; it's like splitting hairs. That's how close a win is at her performance level.

Lindsey shakes her head, breaking through Micah's

thoughts, and says, "Running is like oxygen for me. I don't want to stop."

And slowing down would be death. He knows it, too.

"So then what is it?"

"Everything else." She rubs her head, pushes her hands through her hair, and frowns when her fingers get caught in it. "I've got to get cleaned up. I'm running late and I have that calc test first thing." She turns away and starts closing the door.

"You want to ride in with me and Viv?" he offers.

But she shakes her head. "Dad will drive me."

"What's this about Dad?"

They didn't hear him approach. Usually their father is in the kitchen this early in the morning, preparing the breakfast of champions.

Micah turns. Dad is cresting the stairs, holding a cardboard box labeled *Christmas*. They took the tree down a week ago, but the boxes of decorations have been stacked in the living room, waiting to be hauled up to the attic.

"You'll drive me to school." Lindsey fills him in.

"Each and every morning. Without fail."

He's like that with Lindsey, Micah thinks, a little controlling. More than a little protective. She has no space. If their father isn't standing over her, Coach Kelley is. It would make Micah claustrophobic, and he wonders how Lindsey feels about having no freedom—*at all*.

"She can ride in with me," Micah says again.

"Not necessary," their father says. "My gas tank is full, and this morning, my schedule is empty." He hands the box to Micah. "Take this up," he says, nodding toward the attic.

Then he turns to Lindsey, and the smile slips off his face. She looks more like Hägar the Horrible than Hercules. "You need to get a move on. You've been pretty sluggish the last few mornings. Are you feeling all right?"

"I feel fine," she says.

Illness is not allowed. Their father has a plan for that, and just about everything else. His approach to wellness: vitamins a horse would have trouble choking down, and carefully measured out lean meats and veggies.

But it's worked. So far. Micah and Lindsey are rarely sick.

"I hope so," Dad says, but he moves in, standing so close that Lindsey retreats a step. She puts her hand on the door, like she plans on closing it, but their father is fast.

"No. No. None of that," he says, and makes up the distance she put between them. "If you're sick, I need to know it." He presses his hands to her cheeks, places a palm on her forehead.

And Lindsey is hating it. She turns to petrified wood: a hard outer shell, but completely hollow inside. Like the bones of birds. It's her edge when she's on the track, but Micah has seen her use it with their father before. It's her only defense and it's all about distance.

"No fever," Dad announces.

"Of course not."

He nods, and his voice takes on a tone of warning, "No excuses, then. See you at the table in ten minutes."

And this confuses Micah, because Lindsey never gives excuses.

Their father turns away and heads toward the stairs, but taps the box in Micah's arms as he passes.

"There's another one downstairs," he points out, then descends, his long legs carrying him swiftly into the shadowed well.

"What was that about?" Micah asks.

"San Diego," she says. "It's four weeks away."

Lindsey needs the experience of being on the track with the other hopefuls; she needs the push they'll give her to cut her time. There are three races on her calendar, each chosen for the elite athletes they draw. Olympic Trials are next year.

"I thought you were looking at April, May, and June." San Francisco, Boise, and Baltimore. That was The Plan. It was written down and pinned to the corkboard in the kitchen. Days on the calendar were crossed off. Their father was meticulous about The Plan.

"He changed his mind."

"Why?"

"I'm slipping," she admits, and her eyes are back to liquid. "I'm slower." Her voice is soft and drifts, like a feather, from her lips. She steps back into her bedroom and closes the door, but Micah hears her last words: "I'm losing it."

Micah drops the Alka-Seltzer-like tablet into the beaker and watches the bubbles rise to the surface.

"So far, so good," he says and looks up at his lab partner, shortstop, and sometime sidekick off the field, Reed Daniels.

Reed glances at the stopwatch in his hand and shakes his head. "Not really. The rate of acceleration's too high." He looks up and says, "I didn't see Lindsey this morning."

"She got a late start. She had to retake a calc test and stayed up studying."

Reed nods. His buddy is about nine parts focused, one part worrier. It's a good mix on the field; not so good, though, when the guy is dating your sister.

Micah wasn't happy about it at first—Linds and Reed dating. Sisters are listed under the "no touch" rules of conduct among friends, right after ex-girlfriends. But Micah and Reed go all the way back to Little League, and they have to work together on the field, so he's getting over it. Slowly.

"Yeah. She didn't call me back last night. I thought it had to be something like that."

"I thought you guys weren't serious." Lindsey was up front with Reed: Her life is running. After that, she's all about sea turtles. When she's done marking the world with her Nikes, she wants to become the Jane Goodall of the ocean.

"How can you *not* be serious about Lindsey?" Reed's voice is heavy and a little threaded, like maybe the guy is turning the corner toward desperate.

"I'd say *Ewww*, but I get it." Micah knows how lucky he is to have Vivian. She's the real deal. Something about her puts an air bubble in his chest, keeps his head above water all day. "Vivian's the best thing that's ever happened to me."

"What about baseball?"

Micah taps the side of the beaker, hoping to put a little resistance into the mix and slow down the dissolving tablet. "Different categories."

"Your sister doesn't separate her life like that."

"No." Lindsey is *all* about running. When that's over, she'll be *all* about marine biology.

"It's not healthy," Reed says.

"Really, Dr. Daniels?" Micah's kidding, but when he looks up, his friend's face is all worry. "It's Olympian. She has to be single-minded. It's the only way."

"Time," Reed says and drops the stopwatch on the table. "Seventeen seconds." He picks up the beaker, and heads for the sink, and Micah clears away the remnants of their failed experiment.

That was their fourth attempt. The tablet must take a

minimum of thirty-five seconds to completely dissolve. Micah knows they'll have to add more vegetable oil to the mix and less water, but not how much. Chemistry is a struggle for him. He doesn't understand chemical reactions and doesn't have a clue about how to measure them. This is his second time through chem one. He *needs* to pass this time. You only get one forgiveness in high school.

He heads to the front of the class and takes another tablet from the supply the teacher keeps in a basket on her desk.

"No luck?" Her eyebrow is arched. She's wearing earrings in the triangular alchemist symbol for fire. She's really big on symbols and the periodic table of elements, and the walls are covered with posters bearing their images and atomic numbers.

"I need more than luck," Micah admits.

Mrs. Marino nods. "But I thought you were getting it," she says. "That report you turned in last week was good. Really good."

"I do better when I write about things."

"So maybe you should take a minute and write a little on why you think the experiment isn't working for you."

Micah nods and returns to his desk. He pulls out his journal so that he can at least pretend he's doing as Marino suggested, but the truth is, he doesn't get it, *period*. And the report he turned in last week made about as much sense to him as the space shuttle would to Magellan.

But she's watching him, so Micah writes, *It didn't work because we put too much water into the beaker and too little oil.*

"What are you doing?"

Reed's back. The beaker is empty, and he has a holder with several test tubes in it. Some have water, some oil.

"Trying to figure out why this isn't working."

"We need more oil," Reed offers.

"No kidding, Curie, but how much?"

Reed shrugs. His subject is English. It's Micah's strength, too, but Reed *memorizes* Shakespeare. When he's asked to read aloud in class, he does it like he's living the moment, and not just because he's trying to brownnose some extra points.

"I don't think we can afford to mess this up again," Micah says. He flips back a page, and then two, in his lab journal. "She gave us an equation. We need to use it."

"How?"

Micah is a B student. He gets As in PE, English, Spanish, and history, low Bs in math and science. It all averaged out to give him what he needed for entrance into a top university with a top baseball team. Until chemistry, that is.

He looks across the room. Amber Greene. She's a walking test tube and can predict perfect outcomes before she even mixes solutions. They didn't get to pick their lab partners. Micah and Reed got each other and Amber got Jeremy Poe, aka Peter Parker.

"They know." Micah nods in their direction. "And you speak Poe's language."

"What?"

"He bombed that quiz on *Measure for Measure*. I saw him after school in Eisenberg's classroom last week."

"And you want me to what? Make a trade?"

"Exactly."

Reed thinks about that. "What's in it for me?"

"Your grade." *Obviously*. This is Reed's second time through chem, too.

"What else?" he presses. Micah catches the wheedling tone in his voice.

"What do you want, a lock of Lindsey's hair?" Micah's

joking, but the words clearly hit a soft spot. Reed's face flushes red and his jaw is so tight you can hear the grinding of his teeth.

"I'm not crazy," he says.

"I know, dude. I was just kidding."

Reed nods, but it's a long moment and a few deep breaths before he says, "Maybe you could remind her that there's more to life than running. That she *needs* more than that."

"By *more*, you mean you?"

"Yes."

That's easy. Lindsey does need something more. Some kind of distraction that has nothing to do with running, gold, Kelley, or the London Olympics. And Reed is a good guy.

"Deal," Micah says.

II

1:20 P.M.

Reed leans across the aisle between their seats during trig and whispers, "Did you talk to Lindsey?"

Micah is bent over his notebook, moving numbers around and trying to figure out how much sand is needed to half fill a thirteen-by-twenty-two-by-fifty-foot pit. He spent lunch with Vivian, watching her pick mandarin oranges from her salad and quote her favorite lines from *Othello*. She gave her interpretations, too, and now Micah's pretty sure he'll ace his test next week. But he didn't see Lindsey and didn't have time to look for her.

"About playing Juliet?" Micah asks.

Reed's neck flames. "Very funny."

"I haven't yet, but I will."

"Today?"

"Tonight."

"I asked her to prom," Reed confides. "She said no."

"It's smack in the middle of track season," Micah points out.

"She went last year."

With Jonas Moore. Micah remembers. Lindsey had a thing for the leatherhead for a while, which wasn't like her. Lindsey doesn't go for jocks. She wants a thinker. Someone she can talk to. Someone, she says, who can "connect the dots."

"Isn't it a little early to be thinking about prom?" January is just kicking off, and prom is in April or May.

"I'm a planner," Reed says. True. He's already got a backup list if his first-string colleges don't come through.

"So what if Lindsey can't put the time in now? You know, be a girlfriend? What's your plan then?"

"A," he says, "think positive. B, never give up. C, regroup."

"That's the best you've got?"

Reed shrugs. "I know, pretty lame. But I've already tried sweet-talking, flowers, and attentiveness."

Micah looks up. It must be on his face—the *where the hell did you get* that *from?* look—because Reed says, "*Cosmo*," and blushes. "My sister reads it. It was lying on the couch in the living room, and I picked it up. I guess I was desperate. The article was called, 'Oh, Romance: How to Get Your Guy to Give It to You.' It came with a list the girl can cut out and hand to her guy."

"And it said to send flowers and pull out her chair for her?"

"Those were in the top five," Reed confirms. "The list had twenty possibilities."

"Hit me with another one."

"'Remember When—surprise her with a favorite memory from your early days together.'"

"Yuck."

"Yeah, I didn't like that one, either. And it doesn't really apply to me and Lindsey—we've only been dating three months."

"There's got to be something better than that."

"'Carry a picture of her in your wallet and make sure she knows it.'"

That one works. Vivian likes going through Micah's wallet, looking at photos and holding that single condom packet in the palm of her hand like it's a crystal ball and saying, "Are you feeling lucky?"

"You like that one?" Reed asks, and Micah can hear new hope in his friend's voice. "I don't have a picture of Lindsey."

Before Reed can ask him for one, Micah says, "It only works if *she* gives you the picture and you right there whip out your wallet and make a big deal about sliding it into the first pocket, taking out whatever was there and moving it to the back, you know?"

Reed shakes his head. "Why is this so hard?"

"It's like chemistry. All we need to do is learn the formulas. But they keep changing because every girl is different, and even when you think you know your girl, she surprises you."

"So we're screwed."

"We're challenged," Micah corrects. "Survival of the fittest."

"Primitive."

Micah nods. "I think it's always been this way."

"Girls don't like the caveman thing."

"They do if he's dressed nicely and speaks the language."

"Which means we're right back to the chemistry thing."

"Yep."

"You can smile because you learned the code," Reed points out. "You're not hopeless."

"Vivian taught me," Micah admits, because he remembers wading around in that swamp. "She has a lot of patience and a sense of humor. Both are vital."

"Lindsey has a sense of humor," Reed says, and Micah grimaces.

Lindsey *is* funny—when she pops her head out of the running bubble and lives a little. But sometimes it's like she's a bird hatching from a shell and seeing everything for the first time—it overwhelms her. The image is too sad, and Micah tries to shake it loose.

"She's not the one for you, Reed." Linds still has a lot to learn about guys. Her first date was last year, and that was with Jonas. Their relationship tanked pretty fast. "She doesn't want to be a girlfriend right now."

Reed takes the hit and nods. "She told me that. But she's got to have more than running."

"Lindsey is linear. Right now she's thinking Olympics. After that, it's college. After that, turtles. See what I mean? She's locked in. You need a girl who can change vectors."

"I hate math," Reed says.

"And chemistry," Micah agrees. "But we need both to survive."

Micah walks down the hall and watches the snow swirl in the air outside the windows. He has a free period, study hall during the off-season; come March, he'll be warming up on the field right about now, firing rockets into a leather thimble. He spends a lot of his study periods cruising the halls, running errands. A while ago he delivered some books for Mrs. Ellis, the librarian. She doesn't expect him back; Mr. Tynes, who sent him to the library for an edition of today's paper, does, but he won't make any noise about how long Micah's been gone.

He turns the corner and nearly walks into Lindsey and Kelley. Right away he knows something isn't right. This isn't one of their usual on-the-fly powwows where Kelley slips his sister some words of encouragement or strategies on technique. The air around them is thicker, burns with the words the two of them are exchanging.

"*I* make that decision," Lindsey says, her voice low but insistent. Her back is up against the wall, and Kelley is leaning into her space.

"I do the thinking," Kelley snaps. "That's what your parents pay me for. That's what's going to get you to London." Her voice is knotted with anger. "Or did you think you could get there all by yourself?"

Neither realize that Micah is standing less than two feet away from them. But they're always like that—moving at the speed of light, everyone and everything around them a blur.

Lindsey's voice is trembling, but her chin lifts and she looks Kelley in the eye. "If that's the only way," she says. "But I'll get there."

The words break over Kelley, and the coach seems to freeze from the inside out. She stares at his sister, every muscle in check, but Micah can feel the tension rolling off of her. Then she leans even closer, places a hand against the wall beside Lindsey's head, and tells her, "Without me, you're nobody. I brought out the champion in you." She takes a deep breath, exhales, all the while holding Lindsey's gaze. "You really think you can get anywhere without me? Let's see." She steps back and holds up her hand like a starter's pistol. "Ready. Set. Go."

Then she turns and walks away, down the hall, around the corner, toward the girls' locker room.

Lindsey's teeth start chattering. She wraps her arms around her middle, and her chin sinks into her chest.

"Are you okay?"

His words startle her. Her head swings around, and when

her eyes find him they latch. She lets her breath out, draws another, and then says, "Sure. Just another shining moment." But her voice is thin and breathy and loaded with sarcasm.

"What was that about?" Micah asks, but Lindsey shrugs.

She pushes away from the wall and says, "Walk with me?" Her voice is stronger, but a tear escapes and slides down her cheek.

"Anywhere."

They move in the opposite direction from Kelley and slip out the double doors into an icy wind. They're wearing sweaters, but their coats are hanging inside their lockers. Micah stuffs his hands into the pockets of his jeans.

"I love it out here," Lindsey says, but it's obvious—her face is lifted, glowing, though there's no sun, and she's smiling. "Do you know what this feels like to me? Freedom. That's it. One word, but it's all you need."

It feels cold to Micah. And the snowflakes that looked soft when he was looking at them from inside are actually icy and sting his eyes.

"Do you feel it?" she wants to know, so Micah lets himself be drawn into Lindsey's world, just a little bit.

That's the thing about his sister: It's not just her feet that are gold. It's her whole attitude. She believes—in everything and everyone. No matter what.

"Yeah," he says. He wishes he were a little more like her. The air is helium and there's a lot more sun where she lives.

"That's what running is for me. When you take everything else out of it, that's what's left. She can't take that from me."

"Do you think Kelley is going to cut you loose?" He doesn't think that would be such a bad thing. When their parents hired Kelley to coach Lindsey after school hours, it was supposed to be Saturday mornings only, but Kelley is always around, always intense, always right on top of Linds.

"She needs me," Lindsey says. "As much as I need her."

"Kind of like Jekyll and Hyde?" One can't exist without the other. And the sad thing is, he's only half kidding.

"Not always. I'm not performing right now. Not at my best. She needs to get on me for that."

"Why? What's slowing you down?"

They turn onto the track. It's empty this period, as are the adjacent fields. Without the protection of the building, the wind is at full blast. Micah shivers, and Lindsey notices.

"Are you going soft, little brother?"

"It's, like, minus ten degrees," he protests.

"It's thirty-seven degrees," she corrects. "That's not even freezing."

He turns the conversation back to serious. "Are *you* going soft, Linds? Is that what has Kelley worked up?" And their father crowding her?

Lindsey shakes her head. "I'm tired. I'm in a slump. It's a natural fluctuation of talent." Her explanations sound good, but her tone is unsure, almost like she's trying to convince herself. "A lot of big-bucks, premier athletes go through this. So I'm getting it out of the way early. I'll get my stride back."

"I believe you."

She turns to him, smiling. "You do?"

"Absolutely."

THURSDAY, JANUARY 13, 2011

I

6:00 A.M.

Micah has fallen asleep on the couch, sitting up. Waiting. Gray light seeps into the room; the curtains are open, but someone shut off the light. He hears the gurgle of the coffeemaker and the creaking of a chair in the kitchen. Water is running upstairs; his parents' bathroom. The pipes are old and shriek when the hot is turned on.

"Micah?"

His father, standing at the threshold, watching him. His hair is combed. He wears jeans, a blue sweater, hiking boots. Just another day, but as far as Micah knows, Lindsey is still out there. Lost.

She'll never be found. Not alive. My sister isn't coming home.

And Micah doesn't know how he knows this, only that he believes it like he believes in air.

Last night, Mom and Dad went looking for Lindsey. Their mother talked to Heidi and to Lauren—two "pseudo-friends," Lindsey called them. With so much of her time going into running, she didn't have real BFFs. Mom talked to their parents, too, and called a few others on her cell. But no one saw

Lindsey after she left the Drama Club meeting in the auditorium.

"They said she left in a hurry," their mom told him, "like she had someplace to go. Like maybe someone was waiting for her. She didn't even wash the paint off her hands. Do you know who was waiting for her, Micah?"

But he didn't. And he still knows nothing.

Lindsey had seemed agitated. Worried.

"She tuned out a lot, you know?" Heidi had said. "Like we had to repeat what we were saying to her. More than once. And she kept checking her phone."

For messages. *From whom?* Micah wonders.

Dad came home then, and soon after the police showed up. His mother had called them. They sat and talked in the kitchen with two police officers. The cops took notes and a picture of Lindsey, and left without making promises.

"You're awake, Micah," their father says now, and steps through the shadows. "It's okay, son."

Micah feels the band around his chest loosen. It will never be okay—but maybe, maybe he's wrong. He lets out a breath, then says, "You found Lindsey?"

Dad shakes his head. "No. Not yet. Get up and come to the table. Your mom is taking a shower. When she's done, we're all going to try to piece this thing together. Figure out what was going on with Lindsey yesterday, where she could have gone."

Heaven, Micah thinks. *And she flew there, banking like the birds, her heart a soft beat in her chest, the wind whistling through her lungs.*

"Have you remembered anything?"

Micah shakes his head. He wants to remember, but his

mind is a wide blank screen. It's odd—no people, no scenery, no sound. Just *vacant*.

He doesn't remember Wednesday. His last day with Lindsey.

"You may never," their father says. "Trauma will do that to you, Micah, make your mind a clean slate. It's a coping mechanism."

Dad told Mom that he'd found Micah in their driveway, out cold. That was the first Micah had heard of it, and it didn't feel right.

"Did Vivian drop you off tonight?" Mom had asked.

"I don't think so." Vivian has Vietnamese class on Wednesday afternoons.

"Call her." Mom slid her cell across the table toward him and Micah took it, because he couldn't find his BlackBerry.

Vivian's voice was like an anchor. It was strong and solid, and he could almost feel the earth beneath his feet while he talked to her. And for a moment, memory flickered in front of his eyes. Nothing about Lindsey. It was Vivian. A glimpse of her looking up at him and laughing. He couldn't hear her, but he remembered the feel of her beside him, her arm brushing his, and the peach scent of her hair.

But he was not with Vivian last night.

Mom had taken the phone. "When was the last time you saw Lindsey, Vivian? Was she upset yesterday?"

"She was focused," Vivian had said. Their mother had turned the phone on speaker, and it had seemed to Micah that Vivian's voice was drifting further away from him. "You know how she gets when there's just one thing on her mind. Not much else gets in."

Their mother knew. Lindsey was like that on race day. She

was like that when she had a problem that needed solving.

"Micah," their father prompts now, his voice heavier, sharper. "We're meeting at the kitchen table."

"I need to use the bathroom," Micah says, standing.

Their father nods. He steps back, more in shadow now than light. "Don't keep us waiting. Your mom will be down soon and she wants us to put our heads together, have something to give the police when they get here. We need to know what you know, son."

Nothing. I know nothing. It's like yesterday never was.

Micah turns his back on their father. He takes the stairs rather than use the bathroom off the kitchen. A shower will wake him up. It might even start moving things around in his head—clear the fog—and he might remember.

He pulls his sweatshirt over his head and catches his reflection in the bathroom mirror. The front of his T-shirt is blotted with red and yellow paint—a palm print, off center, with thin, radiant streaks that could have been from fingers.

Lindsey had stayed after school to paint scenery. *Grease.* Were the colors she used the same as those on his shirt?

Yes.

It makes sense. It feels right.

And sucks the air out of the room so that he's struggling for his next breath.

He peels the shirt off his body, climbs out of his jeans. He holds them up and looks for paint. A smear of yellow above a front pocket. The knees are both patched with dirt. Ground in, like he knelt somewhere.

Where was he?

He slides a hand into a pocket and comes up empty. Tries another. And another. In a back pocket he finds a note folded into a triangle, with Lindsey's fancy girl writing: *Personal.*

He opens it.

The unraveling of my life begins.

*September 24th. Bittersweet. Bitter. Sweet.
Bitter.*

Better off dead than alive.

Better running than stuck.

Better half than whole.

September 24th. January 12. June 18.

Days when Lindsey Lost.

Yesterday was January twelfth. What happened to Lindsey? Why was it such a bad day? It wasn't unusual for her to pass him notes in the hall. Sometimes she wanted to talk to him and asked to meet later, but that was usually during track season, when she needed to get psyched for a meet. Usually it was to tell him something. That she was staying after school, so don't wait for her. Once he opened a note that said *Saw Vivian crying in the girls' bathroom. Hope you didn't do something stupid.* He hadn't; Vivian's mom had died two years before and she was really missing her that day. But Lindsey never passed him something that looked like poetry. Like something Bob Dylan could have written. Dark and depressing.

He reads the note again and wonders, *What happened to Lindsey? What could have gone so wrong?*

She'd been fine Tuesday night, the night before last. She

didn't take a call from Reed, but that wasn't unusual—she played hot and cold with him. She'd ignored Kelley, too, refusing to answer her cell or to take the cordless from their father when Kelley had called again. That *was* unusual. As mad as Lindsey sometimes got at Kelley, she never completely shut out her coach.

But yesterday morning she was good to go. She retook the failed calc test and passed. She got a B–, but it was enough that her GPA wouldn't tank. Her scholarship offers remained intact. She'd told him so. They had caught up between classes, briefly, as they were moving in opposite directions.

And then nothing. His memory was wiped out.

There's a tap on the bathroom door, and his mother's voice. "I'm going downstairs, Micah."

She waits for his reply. He can feel her weight behind the door, the air full of expectation. She wants to know more than if he'll be coming, too. She wants to know what he knows.

"I'm taking a shower," he says. He places Lindsey's note on the vanity, rolls his T-shirt up in his jeans, and drops them in the hamper. Then he turns on the shower. The hot only. He's cold. He has no feeling in his fingers or toes, and it's spreading. He can feel the numbness rise above his ankles, seep into his elbows.

"Make it quick," his mother says, her voice harder now, rising above the steady strum of running water.

Micah doesn't answer her. He steps into the tub, under the spray, and lets it scorch him, only it feels like the burn of winter—when it's so cold it won't rain or snow, when the trees creak inside their ice casings and the wind is so slow and thin that it steals the breath right out of your lungs.

While he soaps his chest, he looks for paint that might have bled through his T-shirt, but there's nothing. He moves onto his arms and shoulders, runs the soap down his legs. By the time he steps from the shower, the temperature of the water has turned his skin pink. He dries himself with a hand towel, because that's all that's on the rack.

He has to put his jeans back on to get to his bedroom. His T-shirt falls to the floor, absorbing the water that dripped from his body. He picks it up, holds it from the shoulders, and looks again at the handprint. It can't be his—it's too small— but he checks anyway. He lays the shirt on the vanity and matches his palm against the print. Definitely not, but it could be Lindsey's. He doesn't know anyone else in Drama Club.

Micah folds the T-shirt into a neat square, so that the handprint shows—yellow with some red at the edges around her palm and small fingers.

He takes it into his bedroom, where he changes into clean jeans and a black T-shirt, then downstairs and into the kitchen.

Te police are waiting. Two cops. One wears a uniform; the other wears a suit, a tie, and a shoulder holster. Micah can see the butt of the gun, because the guy's jacket is open. They're drinking coffee.

Micah sits down next to his mother and she puts an arm around his shoulders for a moment. She tries to smile, but she's scared. Her hands are shaking, and when she lifts her coffee cup, some of the creamy liquid sloshes over the side.

That's how he felt yesterday, like an earthquake was erupting inside him. Everything he knew shifted, crumbled, creating an empty landscape.

He remembers feeling, but not fact.

"Hi, Micah," from the cop in the suit. "I'm Detective Bistro." He extends a hand across the table and Micah stares at it before he realizes he's supposed to take it.

The cop's grip is firm, but not painful. He smiles at Micah, but not too much. He waits a moment and no longer before launching into questions that only Micah can answer. And so Micah decides that Bistro is trying too hard to be just right, and that it must be part of his good-cop routine. "When was the last time you saw Lindsey?"

"That I remember?"

Bistro nods. "Your mom and dad told me you're having trouble with your memory. Do you know why?"

"He fell," their father says. "I told you that."

"I know you did, Dr. Hamilton," Bistro says. "Now I want Micah to tell me."

"I don't remember falling," Micah admits.

"What's the last thing you remember after being dropped off at school yesterday morning?"

Micah tells him about passing Lindsey in the hall, about her retake in calc. She was smiling then, relieved.

The rest of yesterday is full of shadow; it's like standing in a dark room, the only light seeping in around the edges of a closed door.

"And after that?" Bistro asks. "What do you remember?"

"Last night," Micah says. "Here in the kitchen, talking about Lindsey being lost."

"That's a whole afternoon gone," Bistro says.

Micah nods. He feels his skin flush from his neck up. Bistro isn't calling Micah a liar; the cop is observing, but it hangs there, waiting for Micah to defend it. Only he has nothing to say.

"Okay, then," Bistro continues. "Sometimes, when you've taken a knock to the noggin, or if you saw something, something you wish you didn't"—he looks at Micah, his eyes *digging* into his—"sometimes you forget. The mind does that for you, keeps it under wraps until you're ready to deal with it."

"You think I know where Lindsey is," Micah says.

"I think it's possible. I'm hoping you can help us with that. Maybe not today. Maybe tomorrow." Bistro sips from his coffee cup, then asks, "You don't remember seeing Lindsey after school yesterday?"

"No."

"The reason I ask, Micah, is because I spoke to Coach Kelley, and she says she saw you talking to Lindsey on the track. That was about three o'clock."

"That's possible," he says slowly. It wouldn't be the first time they'd met on Lindsey's turf. He wonders if he went out there after he read her note. If he tried to help her. He hopes he did.

"But you don't know what the two of you talked about?"

Micah shakes his head.

"Do you know what's been bothering her the past few weeks?" Bistro checks his notes. "Her friends say she was worried, but never said what about. Lindsey failed a math test last week. Her teacher reports that she's never done that before. As and Bs only. Last year, she was president of the Drama Club. This year, sometimes she shows up, sometimes not."

Micah nods, trying to think. Should he show them the note? Or is that getting too much into Lindsey's private thoughts? It's too late to help her. Maybe. But what if he's wrong?

"I found this in my jeans," he says. He offers the note to Bistro.

Their father stands up. "What is it?" he asks.

Mom sits forward, leaning toward Bistro and the note with Lindsey's fancy writing on the outside: *Personal*.

Bistro unfolds it carefully, using only his fingertips. He moves his coffee cup aside and lays the note on the table. The cop in uniform leans in and reads over Bistro's shoulder. Their father walks around the table so he can see better.

"When did she give this to you?" Bistro asks.

But Micah doesn't know. "Yesterday, maybe. I mean, that makes sense, right? How would she know that January twelfth would be a bad day otherwise? Of course, how does she know that June eighteenth will be, too?"

He hates this confusion. It makes him feel slow, lost, out of control.

Bistro leans across the table and taps Micah's hand with the edge of his small notebook.

"It'll come to you," he says. "Usually when you're not trying to get at it."

"But I need to know. If I'm going to help her. If any of us can."

"You sound like it's already too late."

"I don't want it to be," Micah says. He hears the tears in his voice, the breakdown of his words. He wants Lindsey alive, home. But it doesn't seem possible.

"Then let's not give up hope yet," Bistro suggests. "Could be your sister spent the night with some friends. Maybe she's safe and sound, but on her way to see someone. That happens often enough. Kids hop a bus and go visit with family or friends."

But that's not Lindsey. Of course, she hasn't been Lindsey for a while.

"If Lindsey is in trouble, where would she go?"

"To me," Micah says. "She'd come to me first."

"Her younger brother?" Bistro doesn't think so. Micah can tell from his tone.

"By a year. And we"—he pauses, thinking about Lindsey and their conversations—"understand each other."

Bistro nods. "Both athletes. Same parents. Some of the same complaints?"

"What complaints?" their father challenges.

Bistro looks at him. "Usual stuff. No matter how good your relationship is with your kids, they don't like you twenty-four seven. Not when they're teenagers."

"We do have it pretty good, though," Micah counters.

"If everything's okay at home, how about at school, then? Or with Reed—that's her boyfriend, right?"

"Sort of. It's not serious," Micah says.

"Reed thinks it is." Bistro taps the table with his notebook but holds Micah's gaze. "Officers talked to him last night. They said he seemed distraught."

Micah shrugs.

Their mother says, "We all were." Her fingers flutter against the table, almost like she's playing piano keys. "We *are* distraught. We will be until Lindsey is home, safe."

"Okay. Let's get back to possible whereabouts," Bistro suggests. "If she didn't come to you—or if she did"—he nods at the note on the table—"and you weren't able to help her, where would she go?"

"Coach Kelley."

"Are they close?"

"Kelley works with my sister year-round."

"The Olympian and the hopeful," Bistro comments as he makes a note. "They get along well?"

"Yes," their father says.

Micah contradicts him. "Sometimes. Most of the time."

Bistro raises an eyebrow, then looks at Micah. "Tell me about the times they didn't get along."

"She puts a lot of pressure on Lindsey. And it's all the time. She can't even walk through the halls at school without Kelley swooping down on her."

Their father adds, quickly, "She checks in on Lindsey. Sometimes gives her a pep talk. Sometimes a few words on strategy."

"It's all the time," Micah repeats, and he tells them about Tuesday, how Kelley had his sister cornered and Lindsey wasn't liking it.

"What was it about?" Bistro asks.

"I don't know. Lindsey never said." And then he remembers her words to Kelley: *I make that decision.* "It could have been about UCLA. Kelley won't let it go, but Lindsey has her mind made up. USC. It's always been USC."

"USC has an underwater lab," their mother explains. "Lindsey wants to be a marine biologist."

"UCLA never made the list," their father insists. "Kelley campaigned for it, but Lindsey shot it down."

"That didn't matter to Kelley," Micah says. "A couple of weeks ago, Lindsey got a letter. We picked up the mail and went through it as we walked up to the house. The envelope definitely said UCLA."

Micah had been surprised. "I thought UCLA was a dead horse," he had said to Lindsey.

"Kelley doesn't give up."

"She's an Olympian. You don't get there being a quitter."

"I'm not going to UCLA," Lindsey insisted.

"Of course not," Micah agreed. "You're no quitter, either."

Lindsey tore the letter in two without opening it.

"Wow. You're not even going to look?"

"What for? I'm not going."

"What if they offered you a full ride and then some?"

"Nope."

"Gold-plated shoes?"

She smiled. "You can't run in them."

"What if they offer to pick up the entire Olympic tab?"

Lindsey shook her head. "They can't do that. A definite infraction of sporting rules."

"She wasn't going to UCLA, and there was no way Kelley was going to convince her," Micah tells Bistro now. "But she kept trying. She called Linds's cell Tuesday night, and then the landline. Linds wouldn't talk to her."

"That's true," Micah's father concedes. "I didn't know it was about UCLA. Lindsey never said . . ."

Bistro nods, makes a note, then asks Micah, "What did Lindsey say exactly? When she refused to speak to Kelley?"

"'I'm busy,'" Micah says. It had puzzled their father, who stood in front of Lindsey, the cordless in hand.

"Lindsey, it's your coach." Lindsey had shrugged, but didn't look up from her textbook. "You know, that person who's taking you all the way. Nationals. London. Gold."

"I'm not talking to her, Dad." Lindsey lifted her chin and met their father's eyes. "Not now. Maybe not ever."

Then she shut the calc book, picked it up, and left the room.

"UCLA is Coach Kelley's alma mater," their father explains now.

"So are they a package deal?" Bistro asks. "Where one goes, the other follows?"

"Exactly. I knew Kelley applied for the coaching job at UCLA. And USC, too. Athletes stay with their coaches and universities want the top athletes. They want winners. And Kelley's the one to take Lindsey all the way."

"But Lindsey wasn't playing Follow the Leader."

"Not in this," his mother says. "She always listened to Coach Kelley. But not this time."

"USC was that important to her?"

"She's passionate about sea turtles," their mother says. "With USC, she was practically guaranteed a summer research position in the Galápagos. Every year." She smiles. "She's so excited about that." Her voice breaks, and Micah turns to watch her, wondering if this is the way he'll see everything now—in pieces—because their mother's face seems to be separating, each feature breaking away from the whole in some kind of free-float.

Dad moves behind her, rests his hands on her shoulders, pulls her back toward him.

"Lindsey believes she can have everything," his father adds. "And she doesn't mind working harder for it."

Bistro digests this, scratches a few words into his notebook, then turns his attention back to Micah. "You know anything else?"

Micah nods, but it's a moment before he speaks. There's no memory to back up what he's going to say, but it feels right.

"I think I saw Lindsey yesterday afternoon," Micah says, and the detective's face sharpens. "I think I went to the auditorium."

"Why do you think that?"

"You don't know that." His father approaches the table. He places his hands on the back of Micah's chair, fingers curling over the wood.

"I think I do." Micah's hands are in his lap, holding onto his T-shirt. "I don't remember being there," he says. "But I have this."

He lays his T-shirt on the table, the handprint showing. His mother chokes on her next breath and reaches for the shirt, but Bistro pulls it away with the end of his pencil. He stares at it for a moment. "It's clean enough. Maybe we can get a print off of it."

Micah feels his father's hands tighten on the chair back. "You didn't tell us about this," he says.

"I didn't know. Not until this morning."

"He was wearing a sweatshirt," their mother says. "He fell asleep in it last night."

"I found him in it," his father adds. His voice is tight, but no longer accusing.

"You got a plastic bag?" Bistro asks the uniform.

"In the car."

"Get it. Get a few of them." He turns back to Micah. "I think you probably did see Lindsey. Maybe not in the auditorium." He shakes his head. "We talked with a lot of the kids who were there yesterday, and with Mrs. Morrow"—the Drama Club adviser—"and none of them mentioned seeing you. So maybe right after?" He tries to prompt a memory, but Micah is still blank. "It's important, Micah, because you might be the last person who saw your sister yesterday."

"But I don't know," Micah says.

Bistro turns to Micah's father. "Of course, you reported that you found Micah around three thirty. And Lindsey didn't leave Drama Club until four ten. That's a big conflict in time."

"I said four, maybe four thirty," Dad says, and Bistro flips back through his notebook.

"Hmm. There must have been some confusion. The notes I have from the first officer on scene last night reported that you found Micah at three thirty." Bistro taps his notebook with the pencil. "At the end of your driveway."

"I'm sure I said four thirty. What does it matter, anyway?"

"Chain of events, Dr. Hamilton. Micah couldn't have been at the auditorium at four ten, when your daughter left, if he was here. Unconscious."

"Micah, honey, we need you to remember," his mom says, her voice teary. "You may have been the last one to see Lindsey. Maybe you know where she went? Maybe she told you she was going somewhere . . . What she was upset about?" Her hand covers Micah's and she gives it a squeeze. "Please, honey, try."

"I *am* trying, Mom," he says. "I want to remember."

And every time he goes there, steps backward in his mind, it's a complete whiteout. Only there's something beyond memory, something dark and crouching, and Micah wants nothing to do with it. Whenever he gets close, his heart kicks into overdrive, makes him gasp for breath, makes him want to run.

Bistro flips to a clean page in his notebook and gains Micah's attention. "Why don't you tell me how Lindsey usually got home from school."

"We already did that," Micah's father points out.

"You have, Dr. Hamilton. Your wife has," Bistro says patiently. "But Micah hasn't, and I think he probably knows better than either of you how your daughter got home most days."

"She ran," Micah says, grasping the line. "She liked that, even when it was cold."

Bistro makes a note. "Then she kept to the surface streets?"

Micah shook his head. "She liked taking Twin Ferry Road. And she cut through the apple orchard a lot, the north side."

"That apple orchard, whose is it?" asks Bistro, looking at the cop in uniform.

"Bryce's Farm," the uniform says.

"I already followed her route home," Micah's father insists. "I drove it four times last night and again early this morning."

"Well, another set of eyes won't hurt." Bistro rises. "Work on that memory," he says to Micah. "Sometimes it comes back in pieces."

"And sometimes not at all," Micah's father cuts in. "Sometimes, with trauma to the head, the victim never has total recall."

Bistro shrugs. "That hasn't been my experience."

"But I'm a doctor—a psychiatrist—and you're not," Dad points out. "I've had more than a few patients with missing pieces."

"You don't want your son remembering?"

Dad pauses. "I don't want him under that kind of pressure, waiting, hoping. . . . Sometimes the brain shuts down as a defense mechanism. As a matter of survival. That shouldn't be pushed."

"A defense mechanism, Dr. Hamilton? Defense against what?"

Dad holds the cop's gaze. "We may never know," he says, and to Micah, their father's voice sounds like the closing of a door.

III

5:15 P.M.

Micah is sitting at the kitchen table with his mother when his father walks in the back door. A cloud of vapor rises from his head and a thin layer of ice clings to the sleeves of his jacket. The temperature stayed low all day. Now, as the sun is setting, it's dropped another ten degrees. Micah doesn't know firsthand, because he hasn't been outside. But he watched the thermometer—shaped like a Pepsi can—from the kitchen window.

"Anything?" Micah's mother asks.

But his father returned empty. He lifts his arms and his eyes, red and streaming from the cold and wind, go to Micah. "Remember anything?"

Micah shakes his head.

Their father sits down, places his gloved hands on the table so that his palms are flat against the wood and steady. "What does it look like inside your head, Micah?"

"When I think about yesterday? Mostly I see white, like being caught in a blizzard. Fuzzy. Sometimes there are shadows. Flashes of people, but they streak through so fast, I don't know what I'm seeing."

But it's when I'm most afraid, he thinks. *It's when I turn to stone. When my heart knocks against my chest, wanting out.*

"You and Lindsey walked home together," Dad says. "I think we can assume that's true."

"Okay," Micah agrees, because it makes sense. It's what he would do if he wasn't with Vivian.

"But he was with you," his mother interrupts. "Remember, from at least four thirty on."

Time flows around them as they wait for Dad's answer. Lindsey was at the auditorium until four ten; their father found Micah at four, four thirty. He couldn't be in two places at once. And even if Micah traveled at warp speed, he couldn't have made it home in time for his father's discovery.

"I didn't find him in the driveway," Dad says. "It didn't happen that way, Helen."

Mom's lips tremble. "Then where . . . ?"

Micah wonders why his father made up that story, about finding him at the end of the driveway, unconscious. He never believed it, not a hundred percent.

His father doesn't do things like that—lie. But even as Micah's thinking it, a memory unfolds. It was last year, and he was seated on the exam table at the doctor's office. He needed an annual physical so he could play. All the guys needed one. But Micah's shoulder was sore—overworked—and his father was coaching him on what to say:

"You want to play, right? Don't say anything about your shoulder. We can take care of it at home."

"Okay."

"All you need is a little rest. We don't want the doctor benching you an entire season."

Micah definitely didn't want that.

"We'll loosen up your schedule a bit. Less time in the cages— pitchers aren't expected to be sluggers, anyway."

"Sounds good."

"And maybe every third day on the mound until that shoulder's solid." Micah wondered what the coach would say about that. "We have two weeks before spring training. You can ice that arm. Stop lifting for a while. Don't even hold a baseball in that hand until you report."

All good ideas, Micah thought.

When the doctor came in and asked Micah about his "rocket launcher," his father told the guy it was better than ever. "They'll be rewriting the record books again this year."

And Dad had been right. It hadn't seemed like such a bad thing at the time. The lie made it possible for him to play. He had a great season.

So what does his father's lie about Micah's and his own whereabouts do for them? What is his father hiding this time?

What did Micah do?

Micah reconnects with the present when his father reaches across the table and takes his mother's hand.

"I did find him about four thirty," he says. "That part's true." But not at home. "You have to understand, Helen—the paint on his shirt. The police will look at that. They'll know it was Lindsey's hand, her fingerprints." He turns to Micah. "You waited for her outside the auditorium, and when she came out, you talked. Argued, probably. She pushed you away and ran."

"You don't know that," his mother protests.

"I've thought a lot about this, Helen. It fits." He turns to Micah. "What did you argue about?"

"I don't know."

"What was she talking about in her letter?"

The unraveling of my life begins . . .

Micah shakes his head. "I told you, I don't know."

"What about those dates?" his father presses. "What happened on September twenty-fourth?"

"I looked it up," his mother says. "It was a Friday, Richard. She was with you, in Seattle."

At some kind of psych conference, Micah remembers.

"She was fine, I know that," his father says. "Nothing happened. Nothing bad."

"You were at the conference all day, both days. Where was Lindsey?"

Even Micah hears the sharp snap of blame in his mother's voice.

Dad glances at Mom, his face a stiff map of mountains and valleys, then he exhales, a short, shallow breath that thins his voice. "The Space Needle and a harbor cruise, but you *know* this, Helen. Lindsey showed you pictures. And she talked about it, *both* nights, at dinner."

His mother's shoulders tighten. She sits back in her chair, and her voice is packed with challenge. "Maybe she did both on Saturday. Maybe she did none of it. The pictures were scenery. She wasn't in any of them."

"I only know what she told me," his father says, and rubs his face. "You're right, of course. She could have been anywhere, doing anything." He removes his gloves and stuffs them into his jacket pockets. "The police are looking in the orchard." It seems to Micah that each word is punctuated; each an ending; each as airtight as a coffin.

"They looked there last night," his mom says.

"There are more cops today, and they're following a grid. They'll get to every corner. Every inch of the place." He raises his head and looks at Micah. "When was the last time you were in the orchard?"

Micah shrugs. "I don't know. Vivian drives me home a lot—since we took my truck apart, anyway."

"But not yesterday?"

"No."

"So maybe you cut through the orchard yesterday," his father suggests.

But his mother is all about the numbers, the timing and possibility. "How? Where did you find him, Richard?"

"You have to understand, Helen, when I found Micah, he was"—his father spreads his hands as he searches for the right words—"not himself. Not coherent. He was crying. Bleeding. Covered in dirt. He didn't recognize me. He was mentally and emotionally hysterical."

Micah sits back, lets their father's words swirl around him. Crazy. But maybe not wrong.

"Where did you find him?" she repeats.

"He was running out of the orchard. The northeast corner. He cut out of the trees and into the road so fast, I almost hit him."

"The orchard?"

"Okay," Micah says, his heart pumping faster, lighter, because this piece of information feels right. Feels possible. "So maybe Lindsey was with me."

"Maybe she's still there," his father says.

"Did you look for her?" his mother asks. "Did you go into the orchard and *look for her*, Richard?"

"Of course I did. Last night. But it was dark, and in the trees, even darker." He rubs his face again. "I went back today, but the police were there. They wouldn't let me in."

"Lindsey can't still be there. If she is, that would mean—" His mom starts shaking her head. "No. Maybe she was there.

Maybe the two of you argued." She let her eyes fall on Micah. "But she left, just like you did. She got out of there."

His father interrupts. "Something happened in the orchard that's making you forget. Trauma is a strange, morphic animal, Micah. As sinuous as a snake—it can get into everything, change it, give it meaning that was never intended. It's a bull, the way it batters around inside your head, and so stubborn, most patients never regain all the minutes they lost."

His mother stands up, pushing her chair back in the same motion. "Micah is not your patient, Richard."

"He needs to be," his father says. "He needs help. You can see that, Helen. You said yourself this morning, it usually takes a concussion in order to produce memory loss. And he doesn't have one. So explain it to me. What happened that's making him forget?"

But his mother won't give up entirely. She bends toward Micah seeking his gaze, and lays a hand on his arm. "Do you remember anything, honey?"

Vivian walking beside him, laughing; Lindsey, test taken and smiling; and a fist swinging toward him. That's all Micah's remembered so far. He tells his parents that.

"Someone punched you?" his mother says.

"I think so," Micah confirms. "I have a cut inside my mouth. It could have happened like that."

His mother asks him to open up. She takes a look and nods. "Yes. There's a gash on the inside of his cheek. Someone punched you. And maybe that someone . . . maybe he took Lindsey." His mother sinks into tears. She reaches behind her with her hands, finding and falling into her chair.

"Who hit you?" his father asks. "Can you see his face? The jacket he's wearing? Anything?"

"No face," Micah admits. "His coat is dark." Blue, black, maybe green. "The memory is dark, even though it couldn't have been night yet."

"Who would have done that?" his mother presses. "Why?"

"Is Lindsey in the memory?"

Micah shakes his head. "No. I don't see her." *But she's close. Lindsey and a fear so thick, so* everywhere, *Micah knows it could swamp him. There are trees against the sky, their branches stripped clean. The air is wet. And then the arm, a pale fist, and the flash of something metal—a watch?*

And that's it.

"Did you have an argument with someone at school?" his mother wants to know. "Did Lindsey?"

Micah shakes his head. "I don't think so."

"Who would follow you home? Who wanted to see you that badly? Who wanted Lindsey so badly, he took her with him?"

"Took her?" Micah asks. And then it kicks in. His mother thinks he was assaulted. She thinks Lindsey was abducted. But this doesn't feel right, either.

A knock at the front door stops his mother's questioning. She looks at Micah's father.

"Maybe the police," he says.

"Maybe good news," his mother says, but her voice is thin and wavery.

They both rise and go to the door. Micah follows slowly. It's Bistro, and standing behind him is another uniform, different from the one this morning. Their faces are grim and chapped red from the cold. Bistro's talking, but Micah can't hear him. Not every word, anyway. It's like his hearing has poor reception. "Lindsey . . . found . . . dead."

His mother must have made a sound. Her lips are moving.

She folds over into herself, her fingers pressed against her mouth, her face twisted and ghostly. Micah's father catches her.

"My Lindsey," he says.

His mother's crying. Her hands are twisted in his father's shirt. Bistro enters the house, guiding Micah's parents into the living room. The uniform stays on the front porch, the snow over his head swirling in the yellow of the porch light.

Micah can't move. He stares through the window of the storm door, at the cop, the snow, the black night beyond. Someone should let him in. It's cold. Below freezing. The cop's breath flows from his mouth, a cloud that turns quickly to ice. The crystals form in the air and then drift, lilting as they descend toward earth where they will shatter.

Everything that falls breaks.

Lindsey loved the sky, blue or gray or studded with stars.

"It's so big. If someone turned the world upside down," she once said, "we would fall and keep falling and never touch ground." That's what running did for her. Made her feel like she was flying. And when the air was thin in her chest, when her lungs were a hundred percent carbon, running made her feel like she was in one big free fall.

But everyone, eventually, touches ground.

FRIDAY, JANUARY 14, 2011-
TUESDAY, JANUARY 18, 2011

I

Micah's grandfather arrives just as the sun is setting. He drove himself from the airport in a rented
Mazda3 that slides on a patch of ice before it begins
the arduous climb up the gravel driveway. Micah stands on
the front porch, his hands stuffed into the front pockets of
his jeans, and lets the wind rip through his T-shirt. Above
him, the sky roils with clouds the color and texture of a
dove's breast. More snow. The Cascade Range is a bumpy,
scalloped ridge of rock and fertile soil, with small valley
pockets completely at the mercy of mountain weather.

His grandfather had called from the airport.

"I expect it'll be an hour drive stretched into two, two and
a half hours." An ice storm rushed through in the early morning, and the temperature hovered all afternoon at freezing.
There was no melt. "How's your mother, Micah?"

"Holding up," Micah said. Their mom is slow to rise in the
morning, and more than once since Lindsey died he's found
her sitting at the kitchen table, in the muted track lighting,
crying. Last night he sat down next to her and she pulled him
into her arms. Her tears chilled his neck.

"Have you cried, Micah?" she asked.

The answer is no. Not yet. The tears are stuck in his throat, heavy, the pressure increasing. He'll cry, but he doesn't know when.

"You seem stunned still, frozen," she said.

And that's exactly how he feels. Lost in that cloudy moment of realization: *Lindsey is dead.* And not able to escape from the idea that he might have done it.

His father thinks so.

He hasn't said as much. He wants Micah to remember on his own. At odd moments, his father steps out of the shadows of the hallway or the den and asks, "Anything yet?" Or comments, "It'll come to you. Some part of it will, anyway." He has explained how suppressed memory works: "Like a puzzle. One piece at a time. And probably not all of it. The worst, the most unacceptable moment, is lost forever."

He wouldn't let Micah talk to the police. "There's no need. Not yet. Not until you remember." He ran his hand over Micah's head and let it rest on his shoulder. "When you remember, and we talk about it, get it straight, then you can tell the police what you know."

Micah nodded.

"I don't want anyone telling you what to remember. Or even suggesting it."

His father thinks he killed Lindsey, and that pulls Micah's heart into a tight knot in his chest. How can his father think that, if it isn't true? If he doesn't *know*?

"Micah!" His grandfather's bellow reaches his ears and scatters his thoughts. The old man is already at the back of the car, the trunk popped.

Micah makes it to his side in time to wrestle his suitcase away. "Let me, Grandpa."

His grandfather releases the case, but only so he can place

a hand on Micah's arm. His grandfather is a big man, still stands tall and sturdy, and he has a calm about him that Micah supposes comes from having lived it all: a war, the loss of his wife and his son. That calm seeps through his grandfather's hand and into Micah's porous skin. A warm, steady flow of certainty.

"I'm sorry, son," his grandfather says.

At this moment, Micah feels the closest to tears yet. He nods, tries to clear his throat but can't, so he just nods again and turns toward the house.

Dad is at the funeral home. Right before he left, he asked Mom the name of Lindsey's favorite flower.

"Can you believe I don't know that?" he said. "How could I not know that?"

"You do know it," Mom said. "You came home with a dozen calla lilies last year on her birthday."

His father's face went from pained to full relief. "Yeah, I did. I did that." He walked out the back door, murmuring, "Calla lilies."

And his mother turned to Micah and said, "It's terrifying, forgetting."

But he doesn't think he'll ever forget anything about Lindsey. He won't let himself. And that includes the moments his brain is hiding.

"Is your mom here, Micah?"

He drops his grandfather's suitcase at the bottom of the staircase. When he turns around, he realizes that none of the lights is on; his grandfather stands in the center of the living room in shadow, slipping out of his parka.

"She's in Lindsey's room. She was supposed to pick out an outfit for her, you know, to be buried in," Micah explains. "They wanted it today, but Mom can't figure it out."

Dad told her to choose a sweater, a turtleneck to cover the bruises and the empty place where Lindsey's necklace should be—the police didn't find it. Mom and Dad asked, and Bistro looked through the evidence collected from the scene, but it wasn't there.

The necklace was a charm of Mercury's foot dangling on a silver chain. Their father gave it to her after Nationals, and she never took it off. Lindsey could have lost it anywhere in the orchard. Or somewhere before.

"She doesn't like turtlenecks," their mom said, and so she's having a hard time deciding what's right. When he went into the room, she had a skirt and sweater, both the color of plums, spread out on Lindsey's bed. But she was standing over it, shaking her head.

"This is wrong. Your sister didn't even like this outfit." She turned to him. "Remember? She said it made her look like she belonged in a fruit bowl." She bent over and swept the garments up in her arms. She dumped them in the laundry basket inside Lindsey's closet, then went through the hangers again.

The funeral will be open casket, and Mom wants Lindsey to look like herself.

"She liked jeans," his mom said. "But is that even appropriate? Is that what she wants? How would she feel about that ten years from now?"

She won't feel anything, Micah thought. *She's dead.*

But he said, "She liked her sweat suit. The blue one." And left the room.

"I'm going to go up, then," his grandfather says now, "see if I can give her a hand."

Micah follows him up the stairs, carrying the suitcase. The guest room is next to Micah's bedroom. His grandfather always stays there when he visits. But he doesn't get that far. As Micah passes Lindsey's room, he hears his mother's sobs, and looks to where she is held, in her father's arms, crying.

Dad picked a shiny casket made of mahogany; an arrangement of fresh orange and white lilies flow over the edges. It's snowing, soft flurries that melt as soon as they touch the wood. Micah stands between his mother and grandfather. Mom's grip on his hand alternates from a mere whisper of contact to a death squeeze. His grandfather's arm brushes Micah's; a few times, the old man places a hand on his shoulder. Micah's father stands on the other side of his mother. His arm is wrapped around her waist. None of them is wearing black, but various shades of gray and blue.

His mother agonized over it, sitting on the edge of her bed with the blinds drawn and the overhead light dimmed. "I don't have anything to wear," she'd said. "Nothing appropriate."

"No one is ever prepared for something like this," said Grandpa. He sorted through the dresses on the bed and chose the navy. "I think this one is fine. Wasn't blue Lindsey's favorite color?"

Mom dabbed her eyes with a tissue and nodded.

Micah watched from the doorway. His father sat silently in the living room, already in his dark suit.

The preacher makes the sign of the cross, and Micah watches as his mother and grandfather do the same.

They've never gone to church much. When he was younger, they attended services at Christmas and Easter.

With a gentle nudging from his grandfather, Micah follows his parents from the graveside.

He doesn't look up. When they arrived, there were already several rows of people—schoolteachers and teammates, neighbors and colleagues of his parents—arranged in a half circle around the casket. Through the service, he listened to their tears and amens and felt the cool air of their breath on his neck. As they move past them now, they reach out and touch Mom's arm, shake Dad's hand. Micah feels a brief touch on his shoulder, he hears the murmur of his name, and resists both. He climbs into the backseat of their father's Acadia and watches the snow swirl in front of the windshield, over the rolling hills of the cemetery, over Lindsey's casket. His father turns on the wipers and pulls onto the gravel road.

When they reach home, there are cars in the driveway. Micah recognizes a few of them—Lindsey's teammates and their parents, Dad's partner, and a few nurses from the hospital where Mom works. Some of them arranged the food, the invitations, for a small gathering to honor Lindsey.

Kelley is here, too. Her red two-seater is parked at the bottom of the driveway. No way that thing would make the climb without the tires spinning and sliding off the gravel.

As they pass it, memory explodes inside his head.

At first a single, silent frame. *Kelley idling at the side of the road, her window rolled down, her mouth open and paused in midspeech. There's something ugly about her mouth—her lips are pulled back over her teeth like raw scar tissue. Micah and Lindsey are listening.*

Then the image rolls. *Lindsey says something, and Micah pulls on her arm. They step back and Kelley stomps on the gas, the tires spinning and shrieking before they grip the road and she roars off.*

Micah hears only the sound of the tires. He doesn't know the words that were spoken, only that they weren't good.

"Micah?" his grandfather prompts.

But he clings to the memory a moment longer, trying to identify time and place. *Main Street, in front of the coin laundry, not a half mile from school. It's afternoon, January twelfth.* He doesn't remember what Lindsey wore, but he does recognize the tail of his shirt sticking out below his jacket. The T-shirt with Lindsey's handprint.

"Micah?" He returns to the present and realizes they're parked. His grandfather is out of the car and standing in the open door. "We're home, son."

Micah nods. He pulls on the handle of his door and slides out of the SUV. The air is sharp, and his first drag of it makes him cough.

His parents are already at the front door. It's open, and Kelley is standing inside the frame. Snow lands in her dark hair; her hands reach out, close over his mother's small, pale fingers like she's trying to rub some warmth into them.

Kelley can be nice like that. Micah has seen her wrap an arm around a kid's shoulder and give an encouraging squeeze. He's heard her talk about second chances like they're gold. Sometimes, when she talked about Lindsey, her voice was warm, all the way through. She cared about Lindsey, and it was pure. Not polluted by hopes and dreams. Sometimes.

"Micah?" His grandfather again, breaking through his thoughts, and Micah tries to shake himself loose.

"Your girl," his grandfather says, nodding toward the street.

Vivian's car—her Mini Cooper—is slowly negotiating the gravel driveway. Midway, her tires start to spin, and Micah walks downhill to give her a push. The ice and new snow crunch underfoot.

Vivian rolls down her window. "Hey," she says. "That was beautiful."

She means the service, but Micah doesn't remember much of it. He agrees anyway. "Yeah." Then bends over and touches his lips briefly to hers. "Thanks for coming."

It wasn't easy for her; she didn't say as much, but last night she picked him up and they drove for hours, Micah mostly silent and Vivian talking a lot about her mom. The stuff they did together; the secrets they shared. But she frowns now and says, "Duh, of course," in a tone that is soft and all about supporting him.

Micah smiles, and it feels good. Some of the cold leaves his body; his fingers and toes tingle.

"Hi, Vivian," Micah's grandfather says, coming up behind him. "It's good to see you again." They met the last time he visited, two months before. Thanksgiving.

Vivian's smile gains a little wattage. "It's good to see you, Mr. Bradshaw." She tells him how sorry she is about losing Lindsey, and his grandfather takes her hand in a warm squeeze.

"How 'bout we give you a hand with this toy car?" his grandfather offers. He walks to the back of the Mini. He and Micah push, and Vivian steps lightly on the accelerator. The little car shoots up the driveway.

"She's beautiful," his grandfather says as they follow. "Shines from the inside out."

Micah agrees. Vivian's the real thing.

The living room is swarming with members of the track team, some teachers, and a few kids from Drama Club. His parents' friends are cloistered in small groups. Mom and Dad are in the kitchen area. Kelley's near the buffet, talking with some of her athletes.

Reed isn't coming. He was at the service, but doesn't feel like "partying."

"It's not a party," Micah had said. "It's just some of Lindsey's teammates, a few friends, coming together to remember Lindsey. To honor her."

But Reed refused.

Micah takes Vivian's hand. His grandfather joins Micah's mother at the table, where she's arranging platters of cold cuts and salads. Her hands flutter in front of her when they aren't touching something. His mother isn't the nervous type, but this is new territory. None of them knows how to survive without Lindsey.

It's possible his mother doesn't want to try.

Mom seems about as substantial as the dust of a dandelion. Dad vacillates; when he isn't all about Micah, he sits in the corner shadows of their home, as dark and lost as a sunken ship. And Micah himself is an amnesiac.

Vivian goes to fix a single plate for both of them to pick from. When she returns, his father approaches them.

"Hello, Vivian."

"Hi, Dr. Hamilton." She expresses her sadness at Lindsey's passing.

"We're all sad, aren't we, Micah?" His father's voice is thin, sharp—pointed, Micah thinks, at him. Vivian's half smile freezes. "We're having a hard time, Vivian," he continues. "I know you understand that."

"Yes, I do," Vivian says softly.

"Maybe you can help Micah, then. It's not good, bottling up the way he has." Micah feels Vivian's hand tighten on his. "Can you do that, Vivian?" His father leans toward them, and Micah picks up the scent of alcohol on his breath. "Get him to talk about how he feels. Get him to cry a little. Laugh a little.

You know, normal emotions for a time like this. It's important that Micah remember his sister."

"He hasn't forgotten her, sir," Vivian says.

"Actually, he has," his father corrects. "Hasn't Micah told you? He doesn't remember Wednesday, January twelfth. Not at all." And then he turns, unsteady on his feet, and walks away, his body tilted forward like he's walking into a heavy wind. He's overcorrecting.

"Wow," Vivian breathes.

"He's been drinking," Micah says. Which doesn't happen often. His parents are strictly wine and beer, and not much of either. "It's true, though. I don't remember the day Lindsey died. I was with her. Maybe I was the last person to see her, and I don't remember it."

"You didn't tell me," Vivian says, and Micah wishes he had. Last night would have been the perfect time, when she was talking about losing her mother. She slipped away with Vivian sitting beside her bed, and that meant something. Those moments are like precious stones to her, that she can hold, carry with her everywhere, never part with. So how could Micah tell her that he was with Lindsey and remembered nothing of what she found so sacred?

He tries anyway, and tells her about Lindsey's handprint on his shirt and how Micah's father found him, either running like a bat out of hell from the orchard, where Lindsey's body was later discovered, or unconscious at the end of their driveway.

"He lied about it?" Vivian's eyebrows shoot upward.

Micah shrugs. "I think he was trying to protect me."

She lets that rest, but asks him about the paint. "You don't remember going to Drama Club? Seeing Lindsey?"

"I don't even remember saying good-bye to you that afternoon," Micah admits.

"You did," she says. "You walked me to my car, and we stood there for a few minutes talking . . ." She waits, her face open and hopeful, but Micah shakes his head.

"Nothing," he says.

A frown dips between her eyebrows.

"You were headed to the cages after that," she tries. "Did you get there?"

"I don't think so," he says. "I remember the orchard. My father was right about that. I know I was there." He closes his eyes and rolls the brief clip of a hand swinging toward him and the bare, gnarled apple trees rising around him. "But my father didn't tell me that. In the beginning, he wouldn't tell me anything at all."

"Do you think your father is hiding something?"

"Me," Micah says. "He's trying to protect me."

"From what?"

"He thinks I killed Lindsey."

And Vivian's eyes flare in a clutch moment that quickly fades. Color fills her cheeks. Her lips purse before she launches into her argument. "No way," she says. "You guys loved each other."

"I wouldn't hurt Lindsey," Micah agrees. "I don't think I would." But he's afraid of what went on in the orchard and why he can't remember. "Why would I block everything out . . . unless it's true?"

But Vivian is shaking her head. "You don't have it in you. Not for any reason. Not under any circumstances. You're a marshmallow, under all that jock."

Vivian's been telling him that almost since they started

dating. On the mound he's intense, his face set like a Dober-
man. Otherwise he's soft—with animals, with Lindsey, and
especially with Vivian.

"You didn't do it, Micah. You told the police about the
paint on your shirt. About the letter Lindsey wrote you," she
points out. "The guilty hide things."

Like your dad.

She doesn't say it, but he hears it in her voice.

Micah doesn't think his father hurt Lindsey. He loved her.
Besides, his father doesn't blow his horn in traffic; he carries
bugs outside; he spreads bar soap in the yard to keep the deer
out of their garden. His father is just as soft as Micah on the
inside.

II

7:35 A.M.

Micah is up before the sun. He stares at the horizon from his bedroom window, standing in a current of wind that blows through the screen and lifts the curtains around him. The cold air seeps through his skin, into his veins; he wishes it would freeze his heart. He once watched a block of ice shatter from the inside out. The fracture lines were deep and all traced back to one point of origin. Another science experiment he didn't understand, until now.

He can just about time sunrise now. He's that good at waking up. He never used to be. But sleep isn't sleep anymore. It's like being inside a kaleidoscope while shards of memory flash and tumble. He doesn't understand the images; he never sees them clearly. They move too fast.

He hears a bedroom door open—the small squeak of hinges—and then booted feet on the stairs.

Probably his grandfather. He's an early riser, up and dressed before dawn. He's a big animal vet. Mostly horses and cows, but out where he lives, in Wyoming, they have wild antelope, and he's seen plenty of those, too.

Micah steps back from the window and searches the shadows in his room for yesterday's shirt. He finds it draped over the chair in front of his desk. He wouldn't have done that. His mom must have come in. Or maybe his dad.

Micah pulls it on and leaves his room. He places his hand on the wall as he descends the staircase. Orange peel. That's what it feels like against his palm. It starts a tickle in his blood that flows straight to his armpit, ricochets off there, and pings his heart. The way fire spreads, fast and furious. And he realizes it's fear.

The touch triggers a memory, first just the sense of something happening, then developing into an image: *Lindsey's face, her cheek pressed into gravel and pocked, feeling against his palm the way the wall feels now. Her eyes are open, but she doesn't see.* The image bursts and the pieces fall like glass.

He held Lindsey's face in his hands. He looked into her eyes, but she was already gone.

The breath turns solid in his lungs, so that for a moment he feels like he's suffocating.

Can that be? Did he find Lindsey? Did he hold her? Did he look in her eyes and know she was dead?

He leans against the wall, but it doesn't help much. His legs are weak and fold under him. He presses his face to his knees, wills his lungs to open, gasps a soggy breath, and realizes he's crying.

Finally. But it's not like the great bursting of a dam. Each tear is pulled out of him like sap from a tree. Slow. Thick. Painful.

It wasn't his grandfather that he heard; Dad is standing at the kitchen sink, running water into the coffeepot. He looks over his shoulder as Micah enters.

"You're up," he says. His voice is pleasant, but not easy,

and as he continues Micah hears a clip to it. "Sit down. I'll make us breakfast and we can talk."

Micah remains in the doorway.

"We need to talk." His father pours the water into the coffeemaker and starts it percolating. "Come on, son," he says, softer. He pulls out a chair for Micah, then goes back to the counter and starts looking through the cabinets. "It's buckwheat pancakes or oatmeal." He doesn't wait for Micah to choose, but takes out the container of Quaker Oats.

Micah sits, but in a chair on the other side of the table, so he can watch his father move around the room; he notices, for the first time, how sharp Dad's elbows are, stark angles against his thermal shirt.

"I'm hoping you remembered more about the orchard. About Lindsey."

I haven't.

"Let's accept that you guys walked home together," he continues. "That you left school and cut through the orchard."

"Because you saw us there together?" His voice is tight, challenging. He wants their father to say it, whatever he knows, whatever he's hiding.

"Because it's what you would normally do on a Wednesday, right?" His father stirs the oatmeal, but turns so that he's looking at him. "So, are you with me?"

"Sounds right so far," Micah agrees.

"It makes sense. All of it. That you started to walk home together. Then maybe she pushed you away—her handprint on your shirt—took off on her own. You knew she was upset, so you followed her. You found her."

Their father pauses and lets his eyes fall on Micah. He feels their weight for a long moment.

The thing is, it *does* make sense. If Dad found him tearing out of the orchard, not far from where the police found Lindsey's body. If the memory that exploded inside his head this morning is fact.

"Okay," Micah says.

His father puts down the wooden spoon and approaches the table. "Memory is funny," he says. "And pretty convincing sometimes, too. Our minds can manufacture images the way we think things happened." He places his hands on his hips. "I've had a lot of experience with that. A lot of patients who remember things the way they think they should. It's a trap." And he walks back to the stove.

"How can you tell the difference?"

"You can't always. Not on your own. Sometimes it takes a third party. Someone trained in psychotherapy." He stirs the oatmeal, then looks at Micah again. "You shouldn't try to do it yourself. When you start remembering things, come to me. Let me help you." He drops the spoon and sits down at the table. "It'll be scary. You won't want to look at what you're remembering, and you won't be able to trust what you're remembering. That's why I need to be there with you, Micah. I can guide you through it."

"You'll help me? When and if I remember?"

His father nods. "Or Frank." Frank Capelli is his father's partner. "Would you rather talk to Frank?"

Micah shrugs. "Maybe."

"Of course, you're young, your brain is still forming, and something this disturbing—well, you might never fully recover the memory of it."

His father stands and walks back to the stove. He pours the oatmeal into bowls, sprinkles raisins over it, and adds a little milk. He sets Micah's in front of him, and Micah stares at it for a long moment, thinking. His father swings sharply from wanting to know to wanting to bury Micah's memory. And he wonders if his father realizes that.

"Micah?"

His name, even in a hushed tone, still manages to startle him. He bobbles the carburetor he's holding, but manages to catch it before it hits the floor. His grandfather is standing in the door to the garage, wrapped in his coat and cap. His plane takes off in four hours.

"Mind if I come in?"

Micah shrugs. "Sure." His breath collects in the air in front of him, a funnel cloud of frost. The garage isn't heated.

His grandfather nods at the pieces of Micah's F-150 scattered across a white drop cloth on the garage floor. "You going to put that thing back together?"

"I don't know." Not now. He doesn't have the mind for it.

"If I were staying longer, I'd help with it." His grandfather is good with cars, too, and has a 1969 Corvette Stingray he rebuilt from the radials up. He stops at the edge of the cloth, just a few feet shy of Micah. "I feel like I'm leaving too soon."

They buried Lindsey three days ago.

"You have work waiting for you," Micah says, and his grandfather nods.

"I'm worried about your mom." He stuffs his hands in his coat pockets. "And about you, too."

"I'm okay."

But his grandfather is shaking his head. "Of course you're not. You won't be for a while. And *that's* okay. Loss has its own kind of geography," he says, sinking back into his thoughts. "It's a long road, Micah, and not easily traveled."

Yeah, I pretty much feel like I've been stumbling around since Lindsey died.

"You know, there are things I don't remember," his grandfather continues. "And some things are a blur. 'Nam is like that for me now. It needs to be like that so I can get up in the morning, so I can have a life. That's a choice sometimes. If you're lucky."

And some guys, those living in tent cities and pushing shopping carts packed with all they own, see an endless line of the walking dead. Micah read about that in American history.

"You think I don't remember because I saw it happen."

"There's not a doubt in my mind about it. You and Lindsey were solid. Her loss is devastating. The cause unacceptable."

"I want to remember."

"Then you will," his grandfather assures him. "When you're ready."

"I'll never be ready."

"Like I said, sometimes it's a choice."

To live or die.

But Lindsey didn't get to choose. Someone took her life, and that person is lurking inside Micah's mind. What will it cost him to remember?

WEDNESDAY, JANUARY 19, 2011

I

Micah stands in the bathroom, steam fogging the mirror. He wipes a hand across the glass, and for a moment his face appears, water dripping from his hair, into and around his eyes. His lips are chapped, the stubble around his mouth is thick, but he doesn't have it in him to shave this morning. Then clouds form again and his image is only color—the dark brown of his hair—and shape, the sharp line of his cheek and chin. No features. Nothing that would identify him as human. Nothing that would make anyone believe he's still alive.

He wipes away the condensation again and stands perfectly still in front of the mirror, watching for the rise and fall of his chest. Proof of life.

His lungs expand, but the movement is so small, he either missed it or blinked.

He's stuck somewhere between the living and the dead. He's stuck in the orchard with Lindsey.

He picks up the straight pin and inserts it into the pad of his thumb. The blood swells into a single drop and his stomach rolls. But he feels a release, too. Like the slow leak of air from a tire. He doesn't look away. He watches the drop spread, flow, drip from his hand into the sink. It mixes with the running water, turns pink before swirling down the drain.

He's alive and Lindsey is dead.

The dead don't bleed. The heart isn't pumping.

Micah's heart is pounding in his ears.

Blood never bothered him before. Last year, Davey Kaplan took one of Micah's fastballs in the face, tearing cartilage and causing a fountain to spew from his nose. Micah had torn off his shirt and held it to Davey's face while the coach got the first aid box and called for a ride to the hospital.

And Micah was fine. He even got some of Davey's blood on his hands and it didn't bother him. Then. When he thinks about it now, when the image of his blood-streaked hands surfaces inside his mind, it's too much.

Micah bends over at the waist and chucks his breakfast into the toilet.

He tosses the pin in the trash and wipes his mouth with a towel. Then he rolls back onto his heels and braces himself. There's a blood connection between him and what happened in the orchard. He doesn't know this; he feels it. His body reacts to it.

And his father's words confirm it: *He was crying . . . bleeding . . . hysterical.*

He squeezes his thumb and watches the blood bubble and ooze. He holds his hand up, until it's between his face and the mirror—two inches from his nose—and inhales.

Blood smells like different things to different people.

For Micah, it will always smell like sweaty leather and chewing tobacco. Like the fastball that tore apart Davey's face. And now also like apples; too old, too sweet apples.

"Micah?" A soft tapping at the door. A creaking of the wood. His mother is leaning against the frame, maybe has her forehead pressed against it. "You'll be late for school."

She hovers over him now, when the day isn't too heavy. When she isn't slow rising from bed. His grandfather left yesterday, and the house is all shadow again. His father went to work, after sipping coffee and watching Micah over the brim of his cup. Micah feels the tension building inside the house. Like an expanding balloon, at some point it will pop, and he doesn't want to be here when that happens.

"I'll be ready in five minutes," Micah says.

His reaction to blood, to the sudden, thin whistling of a winter sparrow that sounds too much like the voice of a girl in trouble, isn't limited to puking. Sometimes his head fills with something like syrup. It clogs his machinery and makes it hard to think.

Sometimes he can't move. His vision is blurred by a bizarre clashing of colors—red, black, the cobalt blue of a summer sky, and white so clear, he can almost see through it.

He wishes it were as easy as wiping condensation from a mirror, that with one swipe he'd see what he needs to see.

His mother's reply is a single word packed with hesitation: "Okay."

She doesn't think Micah is ready to go back to school.

It's been a week since Lindsey disappeared; four days since she was buried.

His mother isn't ready to go back to work. She took a month's leave. Last night he heard Dad tell her maybe she should go back sooner, but slower. A day or two a week, just to get out of the house. To "find a new normal." Mom didn't answer.

Once, she told Micah that more people die at home, or close to it, than in the ER. Now he believes it.

Bryce's Orchard is less than a mile from their house.

Seven-tenths of a mile from the end of the driveway. He measured it with the odometer of his mother's car. Close enough that it's almost home.

He watches the strip of light under the door, her shadow disappearing as she moves away, then he turns back to the mirror and leans closer. The steam from his shower is gone, and a watery residue clings to the glass.

With his hair still wet and his skin damp, it looks like he walked through a downpour.

He stares into the reflection of his eyes, trying to reach past the fog in his brain. He hasn't remembered anything more, but sometimes he catches a glimpse of dark figures moving against a sheet of white. It's like watching shadows play on a wall.

The gash in his mouth healed and his jaw doesn't ache, but a molar is still loose. He works it with his tongue.

Another knock, and then his mother exhales softly.

"I'm starting the car," she says.

"Okay." Micah steps back from the sink and pulls a towel from the rack.

"I put twenty dollars on the counter in the kitchen." She's afraid he won't eat lunch. Last night, she asked him if he wanted her to pack a sandwich for him. He stopped carrying a lunch box years ago.

"Thanks, Mom," he says, then rubs the towel through his hair and over his face. "I'll eat."

A moment later he hears the back door close. He pulls on a pair of jeans and a flannel shirt over a black pocket T. There's supposed to be snow, but he ignores his boots and shoves his feet into an old pair of Nikes. The leather is cracked and streaked with dirt and sweat. The police took his new pair. The pair he was wearing the night Lindsey died. There wasn't blood on them or anything else, but they haven't returned them.

He doesn't want them back anyway.

When Micah slides into the passenger seat, his mom turns to him and says, "If you want to come home, call."

"I will."

"Even if you're there five minutes and you realize it's too soon—"

"I'll call." His eyes linger on his mother's hair. She brushed it today. She put on some makeup, too. Lipstick, anyway. But her face is pale, and the pink on her lips seems to float there, shifting as she talks, like the sail of a boat.

His mother has a loose, drifting quality about her now, and he wonders if she's as lost to him as Lindsey is.

She puts the car in gear and they coast down the gravel driveway, sinking through thin ice into potholes they'll fill when the weather warms. The first weekend of spring is usually a Hamilton family event. His father picks up mulch, seed, and gravel, and they attack the yard, planting and restoring what the winter took from them.

Spring seems like a long time away, and about as out of reach as the sun.

There's a small gasp from his mother, and the car comes to an abrupt stop.

He's thrown forward into the shoulder harness, and asks, "What is it?"

She's staring to the right, through his window, her face as tight as stretched canvas. He follows her gaze. Bryce's Orchard. The sky is gray and the trees are bare, parched to the color of ash from the freeze. Micah's heart stops. His lungs close. And memory unfolds.

The feelings come first: of fear, of running so fast his

lungs burn for air, of reaching. Then he sees his arms extended in front of him, he catches a glimpse of his legs lifting, charging, Lindsey's back fading into the trees in front of him.

Here, at Bryce's Orchard, the sky growing dark, and running through the plumes of his breath, not just toward Lindsey, but away from someone. He's sure of it.

When he surfaces from the memory, he's alone in the car. His mother stopped in the middle of the road and is outside, peering toward the trees. Her hand is at her throat, and Micah can see tears glistening on her cheeks. Then she moves around the car, to the edge of the road and through the strip of grass.

She stops inches from a shrine: a collection of stuffed animals and candles surrounding a white wooden cross. Micah can see Lindsey's name etched into the wood. Some of the animals are jaguars—their school mascot. He notices a white bear with angel wings, and someone left a track jersey—not Lindsey's, though; she was number seven. A framed photo of Lindsey is in there; some smaller snapshots of his sister with some of her teammates are tacked to the cross.

He doesn't get the chance to see more. His mother slides back into the car, rests her fingertips on the steering wheel, and says, "That's nice." Her tears are flowing faster, one drop on top of another. "Really. I'm glad someone did this for Lindsey, aren't you, Micah?" She digs in her coat pocket and pulls out a tissue. "It's so much nicer than the cemetery. I mean, more *alive* than the cemetery."

He knows what she means. When he first realized what it was, he felt her. For a brief moment, Lindsey was here with them.

"It was more than one person," Micah says.

"Yes, you're right. A lot of people loved Lindsey." She nods, and it's one of the strongest gestures he's seen from her since *before*. "That feels good. She feels so lost to me, but that's not really true, is it?" She puts the car in gear and her foot presses gently on the gas pedal. "She touched a lot of people. There's life in that."

They're almost at the school when she glances at him and says, "Are you sure, Micah?" She reaches over and wipes her hand over his cheek. He was crying.

"I'm sure," he says. He wipes his face with the hem of his shirt. By the time he gets into the building, the cold air will have chapped his skin red and made his eyes watery anyway.

There are two other cars idling outside the high school, kids scrambling out and dashing across the frosted grass. His mother pulls to the curb behind them, but Micah sits a moment, looking at the tall brick building. The windows are dulled by condensation, and he knows it will be humid in the halls, the outdoor cold mixing with body heat. W. S. Merwin High School has a distinctive smell that falls somewhere between old sweat and athlete's foot spray.

"Micah—" his mother begins, and it's enough. He knows if he waits any longer, his first day back won't be today.

He opens the door and slides out of the car. He looks at his mom again, but she's put on her sunglasses, and what Micah sees are twin images of himself, backpack swung over his shoulder, his breath forming ice in the air.

"I'll pick you up," she offers.

But Micah shakes his head. "Vivian will drive me."

"Micah—"

But he's in forward motion.

This will be his first day without her since his eighth grade year, when schools separated them.

Micah went online last night, and the kids are talking.

There were parents on there, too. Maybe even some teachers. They wrote about Lindsey and how she was the closest thing to glory that Merwin was likely to get. She ran the mile in four minutes and seventeen seconds.

Micah pitches a shrieking fastball that somehow manages to hit the brakes three inches from home plate. But that paled next to the Olympics.

There was a thread that called Micah out by name. It asked him, for everyone's sake, to confess. Some people wonder if it was jealousy.

Lindsey was a year ahead of him. A senior to his junior. They were both athletes, both competitive—but not against each other, he reminds himself. You can't compare running to pitching, except that they're both fast. Lindsey was as visible as Micah, but less approachable. She was tall, blonde, and super smart. Light to his dark.

But everyone knows the police took his shoes. They took Reed's shoes, too. They're both size elevens. But Micah is the brother, Reed the new boyfriend. And the cops have a Family First attitude.

And maybe that's the problem. They're thinking too much about Micah and his family and not enough about Reed. It's not like a guy never killed his girlfriend before. Or like Reed doesn't have a short fuse. Last year, he launched himself at a slugger from an opposing team, all because the guy told him he sucks dick—Micah's had a lot worse thrown at him and he never left the mound. The fight cleared the benches and finished the game. Merwin took the loss, and Reed suffered a two-game suspension. When Micah asked him about it later, Reed had nothing to say except "He had it coming."

Reed had it bad for Lindsey. It bordered on obsession. So

maybe the cops should look closer at Reed. And maybe Micah will be the one to tell them so.

He starts moving, holding the front doors of the school as his target. Grass crunches under his feet. He lengthens his stride. Noise really gets to him now. He can hear each blade of grass bend; the sound scratches against his eardrums.

His sense of smell is exaggerated, too. Sometimes breathing is like dragging a razor through his nose. When he opens the glass doors and steps inside, he's hit like a body block with the sweat-mixed-with-wintergreen-mixed-with-greasy-potatoes—the cafeteria serves hash brown patties for breakfast—odor he knew would be waiting for him.

Even inside, the cold permeates his skin, slows his heart, reduces his footsteps to a shuffle.

The halls are empty. Silent. He pauses at the foot of the staircase that would take him to chem and debates a trip to the office for a tardy slip. But the secretaries would ooh and aah over him. They would talk about Lindsey. They would probably cry.

He takes the stairs two at a time, but slows down once he reaches the top. Can he sit in absolute silence for six hours while the world spins around him?

"Micah."

The voice is hearty, even at a whisper. Even as it carries a shade of sadness. Mr. Tynes is standing outside his door, his hand on the knob as he prepares to close it.

"Hi, Mr. Tynes." Micah tries to keep walking, but Tynes strides out to meet him. So he stops, but focuses on the open door to chem, two classrooms down.

"I'm sorry, Micah. If you need anything—"

"Thanks, but I need to get to class. I'm late."

"I don't think that's something for you to worry about today." But he steps out of the way and Micah moves forward again, his pulse beating in his ears, his breath so thick in his throat that he can't swallow.

He walks in as Mrs. Marino is writing a formula on the board. She pauses, the marker in midair, and stares at him. Her eyes fill. Her face melts, so that her features break apart and flow into one another.

II

11:20 A.M.

Micah watches the red second hand on the clock shudder through the final moments of world history. He took notes at the beginning of class, but then Mr. Streeter put a movie on and Micah fell inward, away from the blood and the explosions of war. On the screen, the Carthaginians surged into battle; inside Micah, a band of emotions clashed.

Fear and fire.

Hot and cold.

Did I kill Lindsey?

He slips his hand into his pocket and fumbles with the metal stabber, a knot of nails he twisted into a cyclone the night before. He presses his index finger against it, and it's like touching a hot poker—a small burn followed by a thin, sharp ribbon of release. He doesn't know how they're connected, but as soon as he lets the blood out, his chest eases, his lungs open, and he can breathe again. The darkness crowding the edges of his vision recedes. *Pain,* he thinks, *is proof of life.*

He wants to remember the last words he spoke to his sister.

Did they argue? Coach Kelley told the police they did. They stood on the grass, surrounded by the black tar track and a straggle of halfhearted runners, and spoke loud enough that Kelley heard their voices—but not their words. She watched Lindsey back away from Micah, turn and sprint down the inside lane, and Micah walk off the track and into the student parking lot.

All possible. It sounds right. It even feels right.

He worries about his mother alone in the house.

She passes through the rooms, laying her hands on the walls. Sometimes she hovers in a doorway, just her fingertips pressed to the frame. His mother is fading; his father is waiting; and Micah is suspended between them.

"Micah?"

His name, spoken slowly because everyone knows he's not the same kid he was a week ago, hits his ears like a firecracker. His shoulders flinch, his eyes snap, before he reminds himself: *I'm in school, history class, alive.*

Mr. Streeter is standing in front of his desk.

"Class is over," Streeter says, and Micah looks around him. The other desks are empty.

Micah closes his notebook and slips it into his backpack. He doesn't look into the teacher's face. They're all the same, anyway: soft, worried, poised to say something that will only make Micah wish he were deeper than his sister's six feet under.

He's almost to the door when Streeter says, "Fourth period," like Micah's completely lost his grip on time and place.

He passes through the door, into the crowded hall, without saying anything, without looking back.

Don't look back.

That was the advice the counselor gave when she called him into her office earlier. "Don't look back at . . . *it.* Remember Lindsey, keep her here." The woman patted her chest over the swirling blue pattern of flowers on her shirt and over her heart. "Think about her life, not her death."

Like Micah could just skip over that part. Like if he could forget it, then it never really happened.

There's one image he can't stop from playing in front of his eyes. It happens in his sleep and when he's awake.

Lindsey lying in the orchard.

The ground is covered in places with snow. Leaves, brown, oval, brittle, skitter across her body. She isn't wearing her coat. Her face is pale, her lips blue. One hand is curled, her fingers streaked with blood. But her green eyes are already dead—open, staring, reflecting the image of the man who killed her.

But Micah doesn't know who he is. Or even if he's real. The features are distorted in the pupils of her eyes.

Is that memory? Or something his mind created?

He stands now, a rock in the stream of kids who flow around him on their way to class. Some of them look, pass him still looking. He hears his name, spoken softly. He listens to the wave of chatter as it rises and falls around him, an electric buzz to it that is Lindsey's name and his own and the word *dead*.

"Hey, Micah." Vivian's voice is as warm and weightless as sunshine. He turns, and then she's there. Her face lifted, her lips moving into a smile.

He always gets a little rush when he looks at her.

"Hey," he returns, and tugs gently on a lock of her hair. "I like it."

She's dyed it burgundy. She's like that, always changing things up a bit.

"It's called 'Isis Arising.' The color is a little overdone. I mean, a lot of brunettes go burgundy. Next time I'll try a blue tint. Or maybe lavender."

The names fascinate him. Once, he sat beside her on her bed while she went through all her bottles of nail polish. Twenty-seven bottles and no two names even close. To him, pink is pink.

"How's it going?" She knows today is hard for him, that some kids will talk, and it won't all be nice. She read the same web pages and was pissed about some of the comments. She even wrote a few replies that drew some flames.

"So far, so good." No one has said anything to him. Not to his face. A few hellos, and some of the guys on the baseball team approached him. They bumped fists and moved on.

"What are you doing after school?" she asks, and her voice is full of invitation. His mom wants him to see a shrink. Not his father or Frank, but someone trained to handle kids and loss. Grief counseling. She wants them all to go, but especially him. It was his grandfather's idea; Micah heard him talk to Mom about it the evening before he left.

"You're skipping Viet school?" She does this sometimes. He's glad she's willing to do it for him now.

"I could be persuaded."

"I'm doing whatever you're doing," he says. Vivian is like a roller coaster. She has a lot of good ideas, and most of the time Micah likes to hop on and join her for the ride.

"There's still snow on Bald Mountain."

"We can make snow angels," he promises.

"Consider me truant."

Vivian loves snow. In Vietnamese, the word for it is *tuyết*. She told him that, whispered it, like it was something sacred. Micah repeated the word, thinking about swaths of summer clouds and rice paddies. It's how he thought of Vietnam—hot, sultry summers—but he probably got that from movies.

They stop outside her math class. "Meet me in the student parking lot after school?"

The bell rings, and she laughs as she dashes through the door. Micah stands there, watching her slide into her seat, catch his eye, smile, and wave.

He's got English. It's the only class he likes. Mrs. Eisenberg is decent. She *knows* how to talk to them, how to get them to understand what they're reading and how they feel about it. He walks through the door three minutes late. Everyone already has their books open—*Hamlet*—and there are discussion questions written on the board.

Mrs. Eisenberg's eyebrows pitch upward, but she tells him to take his seat. She usually passes out detention slips.

Micah pauses. He feels like a dartboard, with everyone looking at him.

"I want the tardy, Mrs. Eisenberg," he says.

He wants normal and knows he'll never get it.

"Okay, Micah." She pulls a slip from her desk and writes his name on it. "I'll see you first thing in the morning. And since that's the way you feel about it, I'm also going to remind you that it's important to be in your seat when the bell rings. The rest of us are ready to go."

He takes the slip and says, "Thank you." He means it. He doesn't want her turning on him, too.

And Mrs. Eisenberg gets it. She smiles and nods and tells him, "I think you've taken up enough of our time, don't you?"

"Yeah." Micah takes his seat in the second row and pulls out his copy of *Hamlet*. He leans across the aisle until he can see Reed's open book and the page number. He mumbles, "Thanks, man," but either Reed doesn't hear him or he pretends he doesn't.

Reed wasn't in chem this morning. Micah didn't see him at lunch, either.

And Micah thinks again about the possibility that Reed killed his sister. The day before his sister was murdered, Reed was closing in on desperate.

One day Lindsey took his calls, the next day she didn't. Sometimes they went out and she returned home smiling and drifting like sunshine through the door; other times she was angry, flushed with it, and slammed the door on her way upstairs to her bedroom.

Reed wanted more than she could give him. Lindsey told Micah that. She told Reed, too, but the guy lived in denial.

And the police took his shoes. The thought taunts Micah. He tries to shake it loose, because right now Reed looks like anything but a murderer.

The guy looks like he passed through a meat grinder, which is how Micah feels on the inside.

Reed is serious about everything. School. Baseball. The Seahawks and the space station orbiting the moon. He was seriously in love with Lindsey. Her loss is terminal, and looking at Reed's pale, splotchy face and red eyes, Micah feels the world tilt and his stomach rise.

Reed is destroyed.

III

12:50 P.M.

Micah hears a flushing toilet before he walks through the door of the restroom. He wants to be alone. He managed to get more than halfway through his first day back at school without losing it. The whispers, the stares, are getting to him. He hates the sympathy more than the silence.

Eisenberg's class wasn't so bad, but he can't do trig. He doesn't want to sit there, staring at Reed, wondering if he's a murderer or, almost as bad, feeling sorry for him because he lost Lindsey, too.

He's about to slide into a stall when the other one opens. Reed is standing in it, a ball of tissue in his hand, a fresh coat of red on his face from more crying.

"What are you doing here?" he asks.

"It's a restroom," Micah points out.

"At school, I mean. Why did you come? You don't belong here."

"What are you talking about?"

"There's a jail cell waiting for you." Reed's voice is turning into a rant. He shoves a shoulder into Micah's chest as he blows past him and heads for the sinks. He turns on the tap and bends toward the basin, throwing water in his face. But he's crying, too, with a whine that picks at Micah's skin. "Why did you do it? Kill her? What's wrong with you?"

"I didn't," Micah says. His stomach starts that slow crawl toward his throat. "I didn't kill Lindsey."

"Bullshit." Reed spins around and wipes the water from his face. "Bullshit." He throws his fists into Micah's chest and shoves him back against the stall doors. "The police think you did. They're at your house all the time. I've *seen* them there."

"They've been at your house, too," Micah says. "And they'll be back." He steps closer to Reed, crowding his space. The guy doesn't budge.

"What does that mean? What are you saying, Hamilton?"

"I'm saying you're the boyfriend—or the wannabe boyfriend. Lindsey didn't have a lot of time for you, did she? You hated that."

"She wanted to be with me," Reed insists.

"No, she didn't. She wanted to run. She wanted to win. You didn't fit into her plans."

"That was her fault. I was there for her. I told her I would wait, as long as I had to—"

"And what did she tell you, Reed? Not to waste your time?"

Micah's words knock the last bit of sense out of Reed. He launches himself, planting his head in Micah's gut and taking him down to the floor.

"I wasn't a waste of her time," he shouts. "She was a waste of *my* time."

"They took your shoes. What did they find on them?"

"Nothing!"

Micah is bigger, taller, and turns so that he has Reed pinned to the floor.

"Did you kill her?"

"I loved her!" Reed shouts.

"But she didn't love you."

"She would have. She was going to." Reed surges under him, knocking Micah off balance, then places his forearm on Micah's throat, driving him backward until he's against the wall. "She was a loser." Reed spews the words into Micah's face. "A loser. And she lost big-time."

"Fuck you!"

"There are no do-overs where she is. No next time. No tomorrow." Tears and snot are running out of Reed. "She won't be saying no to me again."

"And that's what did it?" Micah takes a hold of Reed's fingers and bends them backward, peeling his arm off his throat. "That's why you killed her?" Micah stands and cocks his arm, but he doesn't get to follow through.

"Boys!" Tynes is in the restroom with them. He grabs Micah's arm and uses his body to shove Micah back against the wall.

Reed stands on his toes to look over Tynes's shoulder into Micah's face. "I didn't kill her," he screams. "But I'm glad someone did."

IV

1:45 P.M.

Micah sits at the exact point on the track where the lanes curve but remain equal. The equat*er*, Lindsey called it. This was her favorite spot during competition. She once told him it was where her feet grew wings. Where she could be abreast of another runner, feel their breath, the piston movements of their arms, and the air stirred by their motions. It was where she found her edge.

Lindsey's mile—four minutes and seventeen seconds—approached Olympic speed. London 2012 was a possibility. She was the only high school athlete in America who had that potential. *Sports Illustrated* ran her picture as an "up-and-coming athlete to watch." It's framed and hangs in her room. Sometimes Micah passes the open door and looks in, and everything about him goes on pause. He can't think. Can't move. And he doesn't know if it's minutes or hours that pass before he breaks loose. Everything is the way she left it. There are clothes hanging over a chair, a pile of textbooks on the floor, a novel—*The Pearl*—open on her bed. She created and printed out a banner from her computer: 2012 LONDON 2012 LONDON 2012. She pinned it to her wall.

Her room is a time capsule.

Because Reed ended her life?

Micah still feels the burn of their fight in the boys' john. Of Reed's words. He believes them. Reed is glad his sister is dead—in a way, it puts the guy out of his misery. Lindsey didn't want to see him anymore, but Reed couldn't walk away.

He tips his head back and draws a deep breath. He wishes this would end, that they could let his sister rest peacefully. More than that, he wishes Lindsey back.

He shifts against the rough surface of the blacktop. The southern face of Mount Hood, capped in snow, and the rugged sketch of the Cascades unfold around him. He tries to remember the last time he felt normal.

January eleventh. He spent the afternoon with Vivian, sitting in her car by the reservoir, agreeing to dance with her father, if that's what it took—Vivian's debut at Viet school is a couple months away. He spent the evening thinking about baseball and whether he'd shave another second or two off his fastball this season. Reed called and told him that Walker Wentz was thrown out of the boys' locker room after wrestling practice, dressed only in his skivvies, and Micah laughed.

He remembers the laughter now as a tear in his chest.

The next day his sister didn't come home.

She left school at four ten, after painting the scenery for the school's production of *Grease.* She stopped at the 7-Eleven for hot cocoa—the guy behind the counter remembers her wrapping her hands around the cup as she walked away; he doesn't remember seeing Micah. And she had her mittens then. She was wearing her hat, a skullcap with reflective tape front and back—an old lady driving home from work remembers seeing Lindsey on the side of the road, inside the white line. Someone was with her. Someone wearing a dark coat and a watch cap. It could have been Micah, or a dozen other guys.

Lindsey always walked, or ran, the two miles home. She liked it. Especially in winter, when the air hurt going down, but had a helium effect on her senses. That's how she described it to him. When she ran, the air in her lungs grew thin. The oxygen hit her blood and floated, and therefore she floated.

That night it took the police ten minutes to ask if Micah's parents thought Lindsey might have run away. They put a lot of soft words around it, but he could hear the doubt in their voices.

Finally, his father said, "Listen, fellas, my daughter is a responsible young lady who would call home if she could. She wouldn't accept a ride from a stranger. She didn't run away. She loves her mother and does a good job of putting up with me. So let's move beyond this."

"Where do you think your daughter is, sir?"

His father lost composure. He covered his face with his hands and drew a breath that was damp with tears, then lifted his head and said, "Maybe she was hit by a car. Maybe they didn't see her. Didn't stop."

It was midnight by then. Lindsey had been missing for eight hours.

"Maybe she's lying on the side of the road, needing help," their mother said.

"We have cars out looking," one of the officers promised.

Micah's father had already driven Lindsey's usual route from school and two other possibilities.

Micah fell asleep that night in the living room with the curtains open. The beating of his heart woke him. It was loud, pounding against his chest so fast it *hurt*.

Lindsey's heart is stronger than this, he thought. *She can go the distance. Whatever's happening to her.*

Only that wasn't true.

The sun rose, barely tinting the sky with pink and blue.

He heard his mother in the kitchen. Crying. And his father, telling her they didn't know anything for sure.

But they did. They knew Lindsey wasn't home. And she never did anything like that. She was three months shy of her eighteenth birthday. She was an athlete and a scholar. She understood rules; she used them like a ladder as she reached for everything she wanted.

Then his mom went upstairs to shower, and his father walked into the living room and watched Micah for a long moment, studying him. He nudged Micah softly with his voice, and when that didn't work, tried encouragement.

Micah found the handprint on his T-shirt, and his father's story of finding Micah unconscious at the end of their driveway began to unravel.

The police questioned it; they speared his father like a fish.

They took Micah's shoes, his shirt, and the note Lindsey passed him and sealed them in plastic bags.

Micah's mom let the police put a Q-tip in her mouth, but his father refused, and he wouldn't let Micah do it, either.

"That doesn't look good," Bistro said.

Micah's father said nothing. He took a card from his wallet and passed it to the cop.

"Lawyer?"

"Friend," his father said. "Lawyer if we need one."

"Micah?"

He doesn't startle. He hears the footsteps, the jingle of keys in a pocket. His trip down memory lane didn't jar loose any new details, but he's still reluctant to let go and settle in the present.

"Micah," the voice persists, this time claiming his attention.

It's Coach Kelley. Her voice is low, no sharp edges—but not exactly soft, either. Athletes can't risk soft. He heard her tell Lindsey that in one of their hallway powwows, maybe a week or two before his sister died.

"You're going soft, Lindsey," she had warned. "And there's nothing worse for an athlete. For us, soft is weak. It's decay. And the only place it'll get you is dead last."

Micah agrees with Kelley. Even now. An athlete must have resolve. Must be determined. Lindsey had that. Up until a few weeks before she died, Lindsey was a hundred percent gold.

He turns his head and stares at the woman, but that's the only acknowledgment he gives.

"Where are you supposed to be?" she asks. The wind lifts her black hair, keeps it aloft. Micah remembers seeing sports footage of Kelley, her arms pumping, hair flying as she rounded the track at the Athens Olympics. She placed fourth; not because a tragic accident stole her glory, but because three other women were faster than she was. And that sucks.

Better to place seventh or eighth, Micah thinks. Better to be grateful for a chance to compete than to be burned by a near medal.

"Fifth period," he says. The remaining minutes of trig. He wonders if Reed made it back to class? If either of them are suspended for fighting? Micah walked away from Tynes and didn't stop walking until he was outside.

Her lips purse as she considers his answer. Kelley is still young. Merwin is her first teaching job. Her first coaching gig. And she had a real winner in Lindsey. Maybe that's it. Maybe everything Kelley touches turns to shit, and they all have her to blame for Lindsey's death.

"Do you have a pass?"

To sit on the track and remember? Hardly.

Micah looks toward Mount Hood. He agrees with Vivian; there is no other peace like that of falling snow.

"Micah."

Kelley's voice fills with that slushy sympathy that makes Micah wish he could shoot arrows out of his mouth.

"I can't leave you out here," she continues.

"I'm not going inside," Micah says.

He never experienced that helium high Lindsey spoke of, but that wasn't all running was for her. There was something like the peace of snow. Of being inside herself and totally out of reach. He hopes, in the end, she had that. That she was able to block out everything happening to her. Block out everything on the outside.

The police say she died from a blow to the head. Above her temple. It fractured her skull. The people at the funeral home covered it with makeup, but Micah saw the purple splotches beneath the camouflage. And on her neck, too. Whoever killed her choked her first.

"Micah." Kelley's voice drops a notch. Micah realized something today: Adults don't know what to do when he refuses. Some let him be: Mrs. Marino didn't ask him to open his textbook or to write down the problems on the board. Others are concerned: Tynes and Streeter gave him space, but watched him. Kelley is worse, though. She's consoling.

"I can't come out here without seeing her," she says, and her voice is more than just agreeing with Micah; it's thin and trembling with memory. "She was the heart of the team."

She was their star. She made the front page of *The Oregonian* sports section seven times last year.

"She was beautiful," Kelley continues. Micah watches her. She's looking past the track, toward the snowcap on Mount Hood, and her face is soft. "She had that quality of light, you know? It's not something you can catch. You can't hold it. But it made her float. It made her shine, too. She smiled, and you felt it."

He knows what she means. And it's moments like these, when he can hear the warmth in Kelley's voice, that he knows she really cared about Lindsey. His sister meant more than just another chance at a medal.

And then he's falling backward into memory again, to Christmas Eve. Their parents had invited Kelley to dinner—the only guest. She arrived with plastic bags filled with Styrofoam containers of veggies and honey-dipped cushie buns—Lindsey's favorite, but absolutely worthless as far as vitamins and consumable energy are concerned.

"It's all right," Kelley said when Lindsey's face opened in surprise. "Every once in a while, you have to treat yourself." Her face was flushed with color, and she was smiling. She meant what she said. She wanted Lindsey to enjoy them.

His sister grabbed the box and opened it, laughing. She offered one to Kelley, who waved it away.

"If I'm going to break one of the ten commandments, it's got to be chocolate."

Lindsey ate and Kelley watched without plucking the sugar out of her hand, or even looking like she wanted to.

The pitch of Kelley's voice sharpens, breaking into his thoughts. She's talking about Lindsey's last day.

"But not that afternoon," Kelley continues, shaking her

head. "She was definitely off that day. Not talking. Not receiving. *Nothing.* I couldn't reach her." She shifts, and the keys in her pocket jingle. Her voice grows distant. "She had a lot of starts and stops, even before you got here. She couldn't get into the zone."

Off-season, his sister hit the track every other day.

"Why?"

Kelley shakes her head. "She said she *felt* her body. And it was getting in her way." When Lindsey ran, her body was absorbed into the air. There was no wind resistance. Nothing to slow her down. Usually. "I never saw her like that before."

His sister was Yoda when it came to focus. The world continued to exist, but it wasn't fast enough to grab hold of her.

"She was here twenty minutes before you showed up. Stayed a few minutes after you left. Then she walked off the track, into the locker room. She didn't stop when I called her. Didn't even turn around."

The day before, when he found them arguing in the hall, Lindsey was still open. She was fired up, but knew things would blow over. *She needs me . . . as much as I need her.* Something happened afterward, something between them that made Lindsey shut Kelley out. Completely.

"She was pissed," Micah says. "At you."

He hears the accusation in his voice, but it doesn't bother him. It doesn't seem to bother Kelley, either. She takes the hit with ease. She shrugs and says, "That's part of the job description. I was her push. Sometimes she resisted."

"Lindsey pushed back."

"Often," Kelley says. "That's the anatomy of a coach/athlete relationship."

"You wouldn't leave her alone about UCLA."

This time he hits a soft spot. Kelley stiffens. Her mouth

thins, but her voice is smooth. "UCLA is my alma mater. Of course I wanted Lindsey to choose it."

"It wasn't on the list," he points out, but she's done with the subject.

"She was mad at you, too. What was that about?"

But he doesn't remember. Usually, he and Lindsey were pretty cool. Sometimes things got in the way, but that was when their seasons overlapped, when they were both under pressure and it was easier to push each other's buttons. Spring training doesn't even start for another six weeks.

"What were you two talking about?"

Micah shrugs.

"It was strange, wasn't it? Her wearing her uniform like that. I forgot to tell the police about that. Maybe you mentioned it?"

"I didn't see her in her uniform." *I didn't see her at all. Did I?*

But Kelley shakes her head. "She was wearing it. I'm sure. She must have dug through the equipment closet for it. They've been packed away for months." She steps back and levels a look at him. "You still don't remember, do you? You were here, Micah. You argued. She said her life was over and you agreed with her."

V

1:55 PM

Micah stands up and staggers. His knees are weak.

"You're lying," he says. The world around him is fading at the edges.

"No, Micah. I heard you."

"You told the police you couldn't hear what we were saying."

"I wasn't sure," Kelley admits now. "But I heard some of it. Those words, definitely."

The trees blend into the sky. Her face begins to look the way Micah's did that morning—colorless and no features.

Beyond that, in the startling light, are answers.

They call to him, move him as a magnet moves metal. But then his stomach heaves. His heart kicks against his chest.

Fear. He's afraid of what he'll see.

He knows Lindsey is dead. What could be worse?

That he did it.

He starts weaving backward, the ground falling away from him, his voice stuttering in his throat. "I don't believe you." The words are a raspy whisper. "I wasn't here. I didn't hurt her."

"We weren't alone, Micah," Kelley says, coming toward

him. "There were other runners. A few kids in the field with the shot put."

An image flashes across Micah's eyes, trailing fire behind it. A boy and a girl—Lindsey's teammates—lining up, balls perched at their shoulders. One leaps forward, twisting like a top, and launches her ball. Then the colors mix, like the flames in a bonfire, blue and orange, yellow and white. They burst in front of his eyes and he feels himself crumble.

When he comes to, Kelley is kneeling beside him but looking east, toward the school. She raises her arm and waves.

"Over here."

Micah pushes himself up onto his elbows.

"Take it easy, Micah," Kelley says. She lays a hand lightly against his chest. "Stay down."

Micah shrugs Kelley's hand off him, rolls onto his knees, and watches a golf cart bear down on them. It's the vice principal and the nurse. Kelley must have called them on her radio—all the coaches and PE teachers carry them—and now she's going to launch into some kind of Florence Nightingale act.

Micah gets to his feet as the cart comes to a stop. The vice principal is out first. She rushes to his side, even as he's backing away. "Sit down," she says. "You're pale." She tries to steer him toward the cart.

The nurse takes hold of his wrist, feels for his pulse. "Feathery."

Sometimes he feels light, hollow, and so small inside himself that his body is a foreign country.

He shakes her off. "I'm fine."

"You fainted," the vice principal says.

"You were out cold," Kelley confirms.

"How long?" the nurse asks.

"I don't know. I found him this way."

What? Kelley's words tear through him. *She's lying. Again. She has to be.*

But suddenly he isn't sure. Did their conversation actually take place, or was it just in his mind? Were the past ten minutes more lost time?

He isn't hanging around to find out. He turns and sprints across the field, leaving them behind, runs over the track and past the bleachers. The student parking lot is a maze of intersecting lines and narrow channels, and he doesn't stop until he's off campus, off the main strip of town. He follows a path he knows well—so well, his body moves without a navigator. His mind is busy, peeling off the layers around what he must know. He gets close, so that the sharp edges of memory begin knocking against the walls of his mind. A headache starts, keeps time with his pulse. And as he digs deeper, presses himself through the fear, he is struck blind by an intense light. Figures move beyond it, undercover, like static on a TV. Voices call out, sharp then muffled. Lindsey's voice. In it Micah hears fear and fight. An answering voice, distorted, and the words so carefully measured out that the tension in them rises and snaps like a dragon. But Micah catches them. *You're dead, Lindsey . . . As good as dead . . .*

He doesn't lose consciousness this time. The whiteout slowly develops color. Overhead, the brown, puzzled pieces of a tree stretch out across a gray-blue sky, and Micah realizes that he must have fallen. That above him now are the apple trees that sheltered his sister's dead body.

"What are you doing here, Micah?"

The words pin him to the cold ground. He recognizes the voice. Bistro. Where did he come from? Was he here all along?

Again, Micah rises on his elbows and draws a slow, even breath.

The cop's standing at his feet, hands on his hips, his coat open. Micah sees the gold badge and the revolver clipped to his leather belt.

"My sister died here," Micah says.

The cop nods. "Yes, she did. Right here."

A chill passes through Micah. He wasn't aware of looking for this place. He was on autopilot. He doesn't remember *knowing* where he was going, only that he needed out. Out of school, out of his own skin.

He didn't even know he could find the exact spot where Lindsey died—did he?

"So, what are you doing here?" the cop asks again.

"Thinking," Micah says. He gets to his feet and faces Bistro.

"About Lindsey?"

"She's all I think about."

"Do you feel closer to her here?" the cop asks.

Micah doesn't think so. He doesn't feel anything here, except cold. It isn't even two thirty, and his breath is collecting in the air in front of him. By five the sky will be dark. Maybe there'll be snow. "No."

"Then why here?" Bistro wants to know. "You can think at home. Or school." He makes a show of looking at his watch. "Why come to the orchard?"

"I don't know." Micah recognizes the antagonism in the man's voice, but doesn't respond to it. He wants to know why, too. "There are answers here," Micah finally says.

"I think so, too. And you're one of those answers. That makes sense, doesn't it?"

"I know something," Micah says. He wishes he could reach for it, that it was stored in a place without teeth.

"What?"

"I can't . . . see it," Micah finishes.

The cop's mouth thins. He exhales through his nose, and Micah watches the twin streaks of steam.

"Where were you the afternoon Lindsey died, Micah? Really? You can't hide behind your father forever. You're sixteen. In some countries that makes you a man."

"I'm trying to remember. I get close, but then it's . . . gone." He passes out or pukes, and the connection is broken.

"Why do you suppose that is? Why can't you remember?"

"I think you're right," Micah admits slowly. "I saw something." *Or did something.* "Something terrible."

"Lindsey dying," Bistro says.

Micah nods. He forces back the tears that sting his eyes, that block his throat, and says, "I think so."

The cop puts his hands into his pants pockets. He rocks back on his heels, jingles some coins, and stares at Micah.

"Your sister sent you a text that afternoon," Bistro tells him. "At three forty-two. We have her phone records. You didn't answer."

"What did it say?"

"We don't know yet. Why don't you tell me?" It's a challenge.

They have her records, but not her phone, and not Micah's, either. He wonders what happened. Did they drop them in the orchard? Did someone take them? Why?

"I would if I could," Micah says.

He wants to. Sometimes he lies perfectly still on his bed, compresses the fear in his heart until it's nothing more than a grain of salt, and opens the door for memory. But it doesn't work.

"You don't remember," Bistro says, his voice sharp enough to leave a print against Micah's skin. He doesn't believe him. "Not even a little bit?"

"No. Not yet."

"Your father made it clear, we're not to talk to you. That doesn't make you look good." Micah nods. "But you cared about your sister," the cop continues. "You gave us that letter, your T-shirt with Lindsey's print on it—it's a definite match, by the way. It makes me think you want to help her."

"I do."

"Talk to your father, Micah. We have a good hypnotist. Someone who can help you remember." Bistro steps back. "You owe it to your sister, right?"

Dad doesn't believe in reactive therapy. He says it does more harm than good.

"I told him I'm fine with it." Micah wants to. He wants to reveal what he knows. If it's possible. Even if what he knows puts him in jail.

Bistro pulls out a pack of cigarettes and shakes one loose. "You smoke, Micah?"

"No."

The cop laughs, but it sounds more like a bark. "That question was off the record." He offers the cigarette to Micah. "Want one?"

"Smoking is suicide."

Bistro nods, but lights up anyway. "Those are strong feelings," he observes after he takes a drag. "Are you one of those people who think cigarettes are more addictive than pot, so pass the weed around?"

"I don't smoke anything."

"Have you ever tried it? Or alcohol?"

Micah holds his gaze. "Never."

"You're a teenager; you've experimented with something," the cop insists. "I'm not going to hold it against you, Micah, unless you were under the influence the night Lindsey died. Unless you tell me it was the drink or the meth that made you do it."

"I'm an athlete," Micah says, but he isn't telling the whole truth. He's tried alcohol: beer and, one time, tequila. The beer was bitter, almost made him puke, but he felt a complete body flush with the tequila. He felt warm and numb.

He wants to chase the chill from his body, feel something more or less than fear and missing Lindsey. He remembers how the alcohol made him carefree, and made him forget things, too, for a while.

It scared him then. But he wonders now: Could it make him remember Lindsey like she's right beside him, living, breathing, *warm*, but not remember that she's gone forever?

The cop nods. "I hear you have a mean fastball, but that's nothing compared to what your sister could do."

"No one could catch her," Micah agrees.

"But someone did. Someone caught her. Killed her. Someone who had a motive for it. Someone close to her. Killers don't choose their weapons; the weapon chooses the killer. Did you know that?"

"No."

"Someone wrapped their hands around Lindsey's throat. That's anger. That's a moment of blinding hate."

Micah feels his pulse flutter in his throat, like the wings of a trapped bird.

"Lindsey lost her balance—marks in the dirt show that much—and she went down, with weight on her. Her attacker stayed with her. That was rage.

"Who could have hated Lindsey that much, Micah?" The cop steps closer, so close the smoke from his cigarette curls up and into Micah's nose. "Who?"

"No one hated Lindsey," he murmurs. His heart accelerates, making his voice thin.

"You're telling me you loved your sister?" Bistro continues. "You're saying you never wanted her gone? Never even thought it for a minute, like when your parents were watching her run instead of sitting at one of your games? Not even then?"

"They didn't do that," Micah says. "They came to my games, too."

Bistro steps back. He flicks his cigarette, only half-smoked, in a wide arc, and Micah watches it hit the ground at the base of a tree.

"Well, that's nice. Your parents didn't play favorites." He pulls the lapels of his jacket close and begins to slowly work the buttons through their holes. Then he looks up at Micah, his gaze steady but less rigid. "But I heard it was your father who really followed Lindsey. He didn't miss a meet. Not even state trials."

Especially not state, Micah thinks. The trials were important, and traveling three hours and staying the weekend in Salem was no big deal. But it's not like Bistro's making it sound.

"My father coached my Little League teams," Micah says. "He didn't put that kind of time into Lindsey." Not until high school, and then he could only play spectator. But he did that grandly. "He felt bad about that."

"You sold your car," Bistro says. "You had a sweet 2006 Cobra, and you cashed it in so Lindsey could chase gold."

"That's right."

"Did you feel good about that?"

"No." He felt anything but good about it.

"It made you mad," Bistro says sympathetically. "It would have made me mad."

"I didn't like doing it," Micah admits, "but I understood."

"The Dream."

"That's right." They all made sacrifices, and that included Lindsey and Micah. Neither sport was cheap; for every meet of Lindsey's, Micah went to baseball camp or put the hours in at the cages. The summer after ninth grade, when it was clear he was on his way, too, Dad hired a guy from the minors as a coach to build up his form and release. It was pretty equal, the way money was spread between him and Lindsey, until the hope of the Olympics.

"What did you do with that anger?" Bistro wants to know.

"I haven't been carrying it around for nine months, if that's what you mean," Micah says. They sold his car in April.

Bistro nods and lets silence gather before he says, "I have a theory, Micah. I think maybe you've been on slow burn. It's not easy being a prop in someone else's dream. Especially when you're used to being the star. Especially when you have talent of your own that's worthy of attention." He rocks back on his heels, but keeps Micah's gaze. "Selling your car and funneling that money into Lindsey's dream, that was adding insult to injury."

"I'm good at what I do," Micah says.

"I know it," Bistro agrees. "Everyone I ask says so."

"I don't need anything else."

"But you'd like it. A little attention from your parents. From your classmates. From the town. But they're busy planning for London 2012."

Micah shakes his head. "When I get on the mound, all

that changes," he says. "We make the papers. The stands are full." And every year Micah breaks a few records. This season, he'll attract the attention he needs—college scouts, and maybe even a few from MLB. "It's like that every year."

"So right now you're just lying low?"

"Right now I'm off-season."

"You have an answer for everything, Micah," Bistro observes, his voice and face flat with disapproval. "Everything but the big question—who killed Lindsey? Why haven't you told me you didn't do it? Usually, a kid your age is blubbering about how innocent he is."

"My sister is dead. I don't think I could do that."

"But you don't know."

"I know." He didn't hurt her. But what if he didn't help her?

"Then what's bugging you?"

"Innocence isn't . . . black-and-white."

Understanding sharpens the detective's features. "No. But guilt is."

VI

4:45 P.M.

The mountain was thinned for lumber, so hiking up its southern face is easy. He and Vivian slip through the sparse trees, zigzagging to keep the climb manageable. Every ten yards or so she scoops a handful of dry snow and packs it into a ball. She got him once in the head—a lucky shot.

"You're not cold?" she asks.

It's after four and the weather, at this elevation, is all about the sun and wind: It's warmer at three thousand feet than at sea level. The sky is more blue than gray, though the edges are beginning to show night, with swaths of purple and indigo on the horizon.

The breeze stirs the snow from the tree branches. It sprays the earth and sparkles in Vivian's hair until her body heat melts it.

She's bundled in a sweater and peacoat. She wears leather gloves the color of Tabasco sauce—Micah gave them to her for Christmas. His hands are bare. His feet are wet and his toes sting from the cold. But it's a good pain.

He tips his head back and lifts his arms until they're circling the sun. "It's sixty degrees." He wonders how close he'd have to travel toward it before he burst into flame.

"The car thermometer said forty-three," she reminds him.

"Close enough."

"You have antifreeze in your veins," she says, and smiles when he almost trips over his feet.

"You know antifreeze?" Vivian doesn't like cars or can openers. Nothing mechanical for her. After high school, she plans to study psychology or cultural anthropology. She's really into people and how they all get along.

"Of course. And when no one's looking, I can read a dipstick," she says.

"You want to learn how to put an engine together?"

"Baby steps," she says.

"We can start with a lawn mower."

She laughs. "How about you come over and make my father's radio work? I'll be your tool girl," she says to clinch the deal.

"When did that go out?"

Mr. Nguyen is all about his kids, putting them through school and making sure they have enough of everything they need, plus a few extras to sweeten their lives. He bought Vivian the Mini, but still walks a mile to the municipal bus stop and rides with a monthly pass. She swears he has two pairs of pants—the same color and style—and a three-pack of flannel shirts he bought in August when the price was sidewalk-sale cheap. His one love is baseball, which he listens to on an old transistor radio. Vivian says it's her turn to give back when she graduates from college. She and Minh, her older brother, plan to buy their father his first new car. Until then, she gives him what he'll allow. Micah wants to do the same.

"A few days ago."

"I'll come over tonight," he offers.

He wants to put off for as long as possible walking through the door into a house that's all shadow because his mother doesn't remember to turn on the lights. Besides, opening day for MLB may be two months away, but Vivian's father likes to listen to *The Diamond Report*, all about the outlook from pre-season and spring training. And if Micah can't fix the radio, he'll have to send away for parts—Mr. Nguyen only accepts gifts at Christmas and on his birthday—and not even a hand-held, bottom-market radio will tempt him. Micah's already tried that.

Vivian smiles and leans into him. She lifts her face like she's waiting for a kiss, but then brings her arm up and rubs a snowy hand through his hair, over his neck and into the collar of his shirt.

Micah pulls back and squirms against the glide of ice down his backbone. "That was low," he says.

"You're right." But she's smiling wide enough to melt snow. "You're still coming tonight?"

"Of course, but you have to be tool girl *and* able assistant."

"I thought tool girls can only do one thing."

"Not my kind of tool girl." And he waggles his eyebrows at her.

Vivian's smile wavers.

"Finally," she says. "That moment, you were the before Micah. One hundred percent sweet and salty."

"Yeah." When he's with her, there are moments when he forgets his life is now Ground Zero.

"You skipped trig," she says.

"Yeah."

"You went out by the track. I saw you."

"You did?"

"I went to the bathroom every period," she admits. "I knew

today would be hard for you. That you'd end up out there."

"I can feel her there," Micah says. *See* her. Glimpses. Of her hair, her face, set and determined. Her smile, when she won, reached her eyes and reflected the sun. And then Kelley approached him—

"What was I doing?"

"What?"

"On the track."

"Is this a quiz?"

"Yes, it is," he says. "Provide the winning answer and all this can be yours." He spreads his arms wide, but his voice is charged with tension.

Vivian picks up on it. "You were sitting on the track, looking at Mount Hood—until Kelley showed up, anyway. I had to go back to class then, but I'm sure she had a lot to say." And she groans. Kelley gave a woeful speech in the auditorium as part of the school's memorial service. He didn't go, but Vivian told him about it. "Lindsey was gold," Kelley had said. "Solid gold." And she talked about coaching a girl who had every chance in the world of making the big time. The speech ended up being all about what Kelley had lost, and not about who Lindsey was. And Vivian isn't the only one who says so. One thread online was all about the speech; someone even took a photo of Lindsey and replaced her face with Kelley's. "Someone should stitch her mouth shut," Vivian says now.

But Micah surprises her. "She told me something I didn't know. Something about Lindsey, that last day. Something she didn't remember until today."

"What?"

But Micah shrugs. "It's going to sound weird."

"I give an equal ear to weird."

"Lindsey was wearing her uniform. Her track uniform."

Why did she put on her uniform? What was she trying to prove?

"In January?" Vivian frowns.

He nods. "They've been packed away since summer."

"She had to dig for it," Vivian observes.

Something happened that day.

"And then she only stayed on the track for twenty minutes." And wasn't able to focus. *Stops and starts.*

Lindsey knew, even then, that she was in trouble. It shattered her concentration, made it impossible for her to push the world away.

Did she know she was going to die? Micah wonders.

Kelley says so. *"My life is over."*

And the thing is, he can totally hear his sister saying that. If something happened to her running—if she couldn't do it anymore—there'd be no convincing Lindsey that the sun would still rise the next day.

But what would that be? What could take her running but still leave her standing?

Of course, Kelley also told the vice principal she found Micah out cold on the track.

"Where did she go?" Vivian asks. The wind picks up, swirling around them, carrying small shards of ice. She lifts the collar of her coat but continues to look at him with her face open, wondering.

Micah shrugs. "Maybe the auditorium." Bistro gave them a full account of Lindsey's actions that afternoon—what they knew for sure, anyway: She painted a streetlamp for Drama Club. Talked to Heidi and Lauren as she bundled into her coat, but turned down their invitation for dinner. She walked out the side door and into the parking lot—the faculty parking lot, but none of them remembers seeing her leave. No one saw Micah there waiting for her.

"You're right. It's weird that she put on her uniform. She had a reason for doing it, though. Lindsey was driven, but she wasn't crazy. Shorts and a tank top?" Vivian shakes her head. "Whatever her reason, it's probably the clue the police have been looking for."

And Micah didn't think to tell Bistro earlier. He was so warped by his conversation with Kelley, with her bold lying, with the reality that Micah was at the track that last day, that he was in the orchard when Lindsey died.

He has a memory, possibly from that day—of kids and shot puts. And a possible memory, though still hidden in static, of Lindsey fighting for her life.

And he found the exact spot where Lindsey lay dead. He couldn't have done that if he didn't *know*.

He was there.

"There's something else, too," he admits. "I was out there, at the track. I was thinking about Lindsey and about snow, your kind of snow—peaceful, you know—and hoping Lindsey had some of that . . ." He pauses because he can feel the sadness building in his throat. "And Kelley did come out. She talked about Lindsey. About how I was out there that day. She said we were arguing . . ." He shakes his head. "I don't remember that."

"Your dad says it's the trauma. Your memory will come back to you. Some of it. Eventually," Vivian says.

His father's latest theory is that it'll be triggered by a smell or a body gesture; by a conversation, the words or the tone.

And he's right. It's happening.

"I do remember seeing a couple of kids, winding up with the shot put." He closes his eyes, recalls the memory, and adds, "And Lindsey's hair—it was windy and she lifted an arm to get it out of her face. And her breath. The vapor. It was cold." He opens his eyes. "And her shoulder, in the light blue uniform tank top."

"So you *were* there." Vivian gives an encouraging smile. "You *are* remembering."

"But not what we said. Nothing about why she was upset." He stuffs his hands in his pockets and shakes his head. "The thing is," Micah says, "Kelley lied."

He tells her about passing out and coming to with the vice principal and the nurse on their way. He tells her that Kelley told them she found Micah that way—out cold.

Vivian's hand tightens around his. "She said that? You're sure?"

"I'm sure."

"But why?"

"I don't know."

People hide things for a reason. Bistro told him that. And so Micah goes over his conversation with Kelley. Why did she tell the police about the argument Micah and Lindsey had, but not about the uniform?

Because if he really said those words, if he told Lindsey that she was going to die—then he's the natural go-to guy. But the uniform, that's all about running, all about Kelley and her world.

"I think she knows more than we do," he says. "Something about Lindsey, about her running, her future."

"Maybe Lindsey cut her loose. She was always so close, always *there.* I bet Linds got tired of that."

"Maybe," but his voice is more doubt than certainty.

"I don't think it's a big jump, not when you consider she stopped taking Kelley's phone calls."

Micah nods. "Yeah. That wasn't like her." She knew Kelley was her way to the Olympics—someone who breathed that air, who arrived and took the track knowing in less than five minutes she could be standing on the top of the world. She was that close.

Closer than Lindsey ever got.

"My father calls people like Kelley *dữ tợn như chó*. It means *rabid as a dog*."

Kelley is rabid about a lot of things. Her missed opportunity in Athens; Lindsey's promising future. She convinced the school board to approve the funds for a new weight room and a team bus for the school. Kelley was an athlete, world-class, and Micah knows it takes determination, aggression, to get there.

And if she was denied twice—first in Athens and then by Lindsey, if Vivian is right about that—would that make her crazy enough to kill?

Did Kelley kill Lindsey?

Micah's head aches. He feels the burn behind his eyes and his breath catches in his throat. He doesn't want to think about Kelley. He doesn't want to think about Lindsey. For just a few minutes he wants to be the Micah he was before. *Sweet and salty.*

He grabs Vivian's hand and starts running. Stars are beginning to flicker in the sky, and the peak is still a hundred yards' climb. He pulls her along in a lazy Z pattern, and when they reach the top of the mountain, he scans the snowcapped rocks and gullies, glistening under the moon's silver tail, and finds a flat surface.

"Over there." He points to the clearing.

"Snow angels?"

"I promised, didn't I?"

She releases his hand and pulls a flashlight out of her coat pocket. She hands it to him, and then her coat, too.

"What are you doing?"

"They do this in Finland. In Coney Island. In Alaska." She skips across the snow. "You know, those polar bear swimmers?"

She sheds her sweater, her hat and mittens.

"You're going swimming?" he asks dumbly as Vivian pulls her T-shirt over her head. The moonlight casts a silver glow on her shoulders and the lacy bra she's wearing.

"Close enough," she says, and shimmies out of her jeans.

She turns to face him and smiles. Her bra and underwear are no bigger than a bikini—possibly smaller—and Micah forgets all about the cold. Then she crosses her arms over her chest and falls backward.

"You're crazy," he says, but the best kind of crazy he's ever seen. He follows her, shedding his shirt and jeans.

"It's supposed to be thrilling," Vivian calls. "Gets your heart going."

"Oh, my heart's going," he agrees.

Down to his boxers, Micah turns, crosses his arms, and falls backward. It's a free fall that seems to last miles, pillowed on the soft air, on the drafts that carry the birds, seesawing higher, farther, until they vanish.

They lie in the snow, several feet between them, and open their arms, moving them in a wide arc. The snow against his bare skin is first cold, then burns down to a slow sting. And then it's warm. Even the snow spray from the heavy pine and fir is tropical.

He stares at the sky, thinking about how life is all about perspective. He wonders if Lindsey can see them now. Is she smiling? Or is she still caught in the moment when her life was taken from her?

THURSDAY, JANUARY 20–
FRIDAY, JANUARY 21

I

7:15 A.M.

Micah rises before the alarm. He stands in front of the open window, his skin tight from the cold, and watches a streak of blood red burn across the horizon.

Downstairs, the phone rings twice before his father answers it. Micah hears his footsteps on the wood floor, heavier than his mother's whispered shuffling. He hears the deep voice, muted by the space between them. Dad talks on the phone for a few minutes, then hangs up. Micah strains for the sound of his footsteps, for the creaking of the floorboards. Nothing.

And in the silence, he begins to feel the weight of the air. He can *feel* his father thinking, wondering, grasping at possibilities.

He wants to free him from this misery. Confess, so they can move beyond this moment. Move forward, even if it means Micah goes to jail and his father's grief doubles.

But that makes no sense. And anyway, Micah didn't do it. He knows it, in his gut, in his bones, which feel so hollow now, he thinks they could float.

He turns away from the window and pulls on a pair of

jeans, a thermal shirt under his flannel, socks, and his boots. He stops in the bathroom to comb his hair. He watches his reflection as he brushes his teeth. Nothing different. Nothing changed. And that seems wrong.

Lindsey's toothbrush is still in the metal caddy. White and blue. Micah stares at it a moment, then picks it up and drops it in the trash. He tries to put his brush back, but can't. There's something right about the caddy's emptiness, so he tosses his brush, too.

He takes the stairs slowly, letting his hand drift across the wall, hoping to ignite another memory. But nothing comes to him.

His father is waiting in the kitchen. The glass bowl he used for his cereal is set aside. His coffee cup is nearly empty.

"Sit down, Micah."

Another talk. About what? All that he can't remember?

Every day is a repeat of the one before. *Almost,* he reminds himself. There's reason to hope. He remembered more yesterday than all of the other days since Lindsey died, combined. And that's something.

Micah sits, and Dad's hands curl around his coffee cup. "You talked to Coach Kelley yesterday."

"I went out to the field." Lindsey's home away from home. His father doesn't respond right away, and Micah feels compelled to add, "I couldn't sit through trig." *Or study hall.*

"I understand. I knew yesterday would be difficult." He runs his fingers over the rim of the cup. "Kelley just called. She's concerned. She told me you're remembering more."

"I think I was at the track that afternoon. I think I talked to Lindsey."

His father's face is a lot of sharp angles and slopes. It

makes him look angry or stressed most of the time, even when he's anything but. Like right now. Micah can tell that his father is mostly just tired, because his next words are slow and so soft Micah has to reach for them.

"What did you talk about?" he asks, and Micah thinks his father might even be afraid of the question and the answer it will bring. "You and Lindsey?"

"Kelley says we argued, but I don't remember that."

"What *do* you remember?"

"Lindsey needed help." Micah senses this more than knows it. He thinks he read his sister's note and went looking for her.

"What kind of help?"

"I don't know."

"Then tell me what you do know." And Dad's voice is still tentative. Micah doesn't even wonder what he's afraid of—he knows the thought that disturbs his father: *Is my son a murderer?*

So instead he says, "If you'd let them hypnotize me, I'd remember it all. We'd know everything." He can't bring himself to say the words, *You'd know, Dad; you'd know I'm not a killer.*

"It doesn't work, Micah. It's all suggestion. Persuasion. Not true recovery."

"You don't use it?" Micah asks.

"I have," his father admits, and shakes his head. "But it was a mistake. A lot of times patients want so much to remember, or to please someone who wants them to remember, that they're guided by the softest suggestion." His father's frown deepens. "I think you want to remember, Micah, so badly it's blinding you. Sometimes that happens and you just have to leave it alone for a while." He breathes deeply. "I need to be more patient," he says. "And so do you."

"What if I never remember?"

His father turns his hands over, palms up on the table. "Then we'll have to accept it."

But he can't hold Micah's gaze. Dad's eyes glance off him, look past him, focus beyond him. Gradually, the lines around his father's eyes deepen, and Micah realizes he's squinting, as if in pain.

"You think I killed Lindsey," Micah says, though the words drag against his throat, emerge rusty, hoarse. And it costs him. The tears he was able to hold back yesterday stream from his eyes now. His father's hand falls on one of his and tightens. "You do, don't you?"

"You were in the orchard, Micah."

"I know. You told me." *And I remember.*

His father pauses, in some kind of silent battle with himself. And then: "What I didn't tell you"—another pause—"is that Lindsey was there, too. At that moment. There and dead."

Micah pulls away, sinks back into his seat. His voice is thin, airless. "How do you know?"

Tears run down their father's face. "I saw her. After I got you under control, got you in the car, I went back into the orchard." He sniffs loudly and wipes a hand over his cheeks. "You kept saying, 'Lindsey . . . Lindsey . . .' I had to go in there. I had to find her."

"And she was dead?" Micah repeats. The pulse in his throat flutters, making his voice weak, his vision lighter.

"Yes."

"I was with her and she was dead?"

"Yes. And there was no one else in the orchard, not that I could see. But there was a struggle. Lots of footprints, scuffling. And Lindsey."

"I didn't do it, Dad." Micah's tears are hot and fast. "You don't believe me, but I didn't."

"I want to believe you, but who could have done this? Why?"

"Why would *I* have done it?" Micah demands.

But his father is shaking his head. He lifts his hands, palms up and empty. "You wouldn't," he says. "My Micah, my son, wouldn't."

"But I was there," Micah says for him. "And that makes me guilty."

"It shouldn't. You're right." He lifts his coffee cup, but his hand is shaking and the cup slips through his fingers, clattering against the table. "When I think about it clinically, it comes down to one of two things—your traumatic memory loss. You either watched someone kill your sister, or you did it yourself." He struggles through his next breath, then adds, "I didn't see anyone else, Micah. There was no one else there.

"I think it could have been an accident. You didn't mean for Lindsey to die. There was so much anger, and anger sometimes distorts reality."

"When have I been so angry with Lindsey that I'd choke her, Dad? That I'd knock her down and bash in her head?"

Micah's words curl around his father's argument and tighten. His father's shoulders begin to tremble. His hands flatten against the table, pressing into the grain. His pale face twists and breaks open.

"Never. You're right," he chokes out.

"That's a lot of anger, Dad. That's hate." It's hard for Micah to talk, but he pushes through it. *"I didn't hate Lindsey. Ever."*

"You're right. I've never seen that kind of anger in you. I promise you I haven't." His father shakes his head and reaches his hands across the table toward Micah. "You loved your sister."

"So how could you think I'd hurt her?"

"It was finding you like that. You were hysterical, disoriented. And the loss—Lindsey lost like that. And you couldn't remember anything. I kept telling myself you didn't want to remember. Who would? And then it was as if a black hole opened up, and I was standing on the edge of it. If I lost you, too, I would fall. There would be no coming back from that. Not for me. And ever since all I've focused on is keeping you here with me."

He reaches across the table and grabs Micah's hand. "I'm sorry."

"You believe me?"

"I believe *in* you," his father corrects.

"What's the difference?"

"I should have known better. I *do* know better. You're my son. I've known you for sixteen years. I've loved you even longer." His father sits back and wipes his face on his sleeve. "You're a young man of good character. You've always had it." And then he tries to collect himself, to break it down. "Fear can rob a person of rational thought. That's the very essence of the condition. I've been scared from the moment I found you on the side of the road.

"But we're going to find peace. Some way to live . . . without Lindsey. Some way to be a family."

"I want that, too." Micah pushes back his chair and stands up, but he doesn't reach for his backpack or his coat. He doesn't move at all.

"What else did Kelley say?"

His father looks up, meets his eyes. "She said she overheard some of your conversation with Lindsey that day."

"Yeah. She told me that, too."

"But you don't believe her?"

"Linds was wearing her track uniform, did you know that? It was thirty-four degrees. I checked. Why would she be wearing it?"

"Kelley didn't say—"

"Whatever was going on with Lindsey, it had nothing to do with me." His father nods. "I didn't do it, Dad," Micah says again, to make sure his father feels the conviction inside him, to chase away any shred of remaining doubt.

"I know."

Micah shrugs into his coat. He slings his backpack over his shoulder.

"I'm not telling Bistro about finding you at the orchard," his father says. "Not yet."

Because it would make Micah look guilty.

His father stands and places a hand on Micah's head, his palm sliding over his hair and cupping the back of his neck. He makes Micah look at him.

"Inside here," he says, "you're hiding from a killer, from a memory that could destroy you. I won't let that happen."

His father doesn't make a lot of promises, but he's never broken one, either.

II

10:30 A.M.

Micah is on his way to third period—history—when he passes the courtyard and notices Bistro and Kelley sitting at one of the picnic tables, talking. Most of the tables and benches have snowdrifts on them. Except where they're sitting, under the shelter of the second floor balcony, Kelley perched on the edge of the bench and Bistro spread out across from her, his notebook out and a pen in his hand.

He must have felt Micah's stare, because he looks up and waves. It's neither a sarcastic nor a taunting gesture. And the look on his face is different—serious, thoughtful, softer.

Micah moves on without acknowledging the gesture. He takes the stairs two at a time and slips into class as the bell rings. His plans to stay focused, to actually open his textbook, copy notes, answer questions—to perform, so Streeter doesn't feel the need for a "chat"—take a nosedive not ten minutes into the hour, when a kid arrives with a pass. Micah is wanted in the principal's office. *Immediately.*

He thinks about staying put, but Streeter is encouraging him to gather his things and get moving. He thinks about stopping in the bathroom or walking outside into the falling snow, but discards these ideas when he realizes he *wants* to see Bistro. He wants to know what the detective has to say.

Did Kelley tell him about Lindsey wearing her uniform? And what about her lying to the nurse and the vice principal? He wants to know what Bistro thinks about that.

He works the cyclone in his pocket all the way to the office. He pulls his hand from his pocket only after he knows he's drawn blood—the sweet unraveling of tension, the way it seeps from his skin and eases its squeeze on his heart, makes him less afraid.

He's been doing it too much, though. His fingers are pitted, and some days it hurts to hold a pencil. But he can't stop, either. He's tried. The longest he has gone without letting the stress flow is half a day, and by the time he got to that point his blood was barking for release.

When Micah arrives at the principal's office, Bistro's sitting in a chair in front of the desk. His sleeves are rolled up. He wore a parka today, and it's hanging over the only other chair in the room, drying. The principal is nowhere to be seen.

"Have a seat, Micah." Bistro stands up and indicates the vacant chair.

"No, thanks." Micah slides his thumbs through his belt loops and leans back against the door. "I'm not staying."

Not long, anyway.

Bistro nods. "Okay. I'll get right to it, then. I spoke to your mom this morning. We have some new developments in your sister's case. She said it would be all right to talk to you."

Micah feels tension ripple across his shoulders and up his neck. "But you didn't talk to my father."

His father, who believed he was capable of murder, but now just as easily believes in his innocence.

"No, I didn't. We only need permission from one parent."

"What new developments?"

Bistro pockets his notebook and gives Micah his undivided attention. He takes a minute, looking him over, before dropping his bomb.

"Your sister was pregnant. Did you know about that, Micah?"

The words hit him like shrapnel. For a moment, he's convinced that he's bleeding from every pore. And then that feeling of weightlessness happens again. He's so small inside himself that the matter of his body could be held in the palm of a hand. "No way." *Lindsey wouldn't do that. She wouldn't ruin her future like that.*

Those thoughts linger in his head, the words sharp, scratching at some memory—of maybe having said them before?

Ruin. Definitely. He said it, or she did—but when?

"I've ruined it." Lindsey, her voice thin and rising.

"What?" Micah asked, wanting to understand.

"Everything. I've ruined everything." She was crying. Choking on tears.

And then . . . nothing. The sounds seem to flutter, and then fade.

"I'm sorry, Micah," Bistro is saying. "These tests don't lie."

"She was Olympic." But Micah can hear his voice wavering. "She was seriously going places."

Now the questions come fast, like darts. "She was dating Reed Daniels, right?"

"She *just* started dating Reed."

"He's a friend of yours?"

Not anymore. "We're on the baseball team together."

"Younger than Lindsey?"

"We're both juniors."

"A year younger," Bistro says, like he's confirming the info.

"You already know all of this," Micah says.

"That's right, I do. But the perspective of the people around the victim is important. It shows us what they saw, even if it doesn't match up with the evidence. Interpretations can sway the direction of an investigation—do you understand that?"

Micah does. At least, he understands that opinion can weigh as heavy as fact. Bistro is waiting for a response, so he nods.

And then there are more questions: "Who was Lindsey dating before Reed?"

"No one. She was all about running."

"So, she didn't date much?"

"Not really."

"When was the last time she dated someone other than Reed?"

Micah thinks back. "She went to the prom with Jonas Moore last year. They saw each other for a while."

"Where is Jonas now?"

"He's a Husky."

"University of Washington?"

Micah nods. "He's good, too."

"What position?"

"Returns punts, puts some time in on offense."

"Did he come home for Christmas?"

Micah shrugs. "Probably."

"You guys didn't hang out?"

"Different sports. And two years between us."

"Did you notice if Lindsey went out over Christmas break?"

"She saw Reed," Micah says. "She spent a couple days skiing with friends."

"Mount Hood?"

He shakes his head. "Bachelor."

"Did they have a parent chaperone?"

"No. Only girls went. Some from the track team, some from Drama Club. Some of them were already eighteen." It was a big deal. The first time Lindsey was allowed to go away overnight without someone's parent going along.

"Okay. Anything else?" Bistro starts rolling down his sleeves. "Did she see anyone else? Did she go out at night, maybe after everyone was in bed?"

"You mean, did she sneak out to see Jonas?"

"Yes, that's exactly what I mean." Bistro gives him a level look. "Maybe she didn't want anyone to know she was seeing Jonas."

"Our dad would have freaked."

"Why is that?"

Micah tries to remember his father's exact words about Jonas. "Jonas was a dead end." He was a superstar who only knew how to read pigskin. "He dreamed big, like Lindsey, but he didn't spend a lot of time with the books."

"Your father didn't like him?"

"No. But you're wrong about this. Lindsey was honest. She would have cut Reed loose before she saw Jonas again."

"Maybe she tried to do that," Bistro points out. "You said yourself that their relationship was pretty much one-sided." Micah knows he's right. "Would Reed have backed off if Lindsey asked him to?"

He thinks about Reed's list of plays, borrowed from *Cosmo*. About the ugly words he'd spoken in the boys' bathroom. "No. He didn't have a Plan B. He was all about Lindsey."

Bistro pulls out his notebook and writes that down. "Your mom told me Lindsey went to Seattle twice in the fall. One time with your father, when he had a conference there; the second time she went with a group of friends. They took a Greyhound, saw a game, and spent the night."

"That's right. And they *did* have a chaperone for that trip."

"Who was it?"

Micah shrugs. "I think Heidi's dad."

"Do you think she might have gotten some time alone, seen Jonas when she was up there?"

"She could have, if she wanted to, but she didn't tell me that. We didn't talk about that kind of stuff."

"What *did* you talk about?"

"Sports. Dreams. Our parents."

"She was going to win gold and you were going to play for the Mariners?"

"Yeah. But we talked about what it feels like to be really good, you know? How sometimes it's all we are—for me, it's that one raging fastball. For her, it was the moment she blended into the air. When she *was* the wind."

"That's poetic," Bistro says. "Did she say anything about having to give up her dream? Anything recently?"

"The note."

"Yeah. It makes sense now," Bistro says.

"The dates?" Micah asks "How did Lindsey know she was going to die that day?"

"She didn't," Bistro says. "September twenty-fourth was probably the day she conceived. June eighteenth was her due date. We've figured that much out."

Pregnant. Lindsey was going to have a baby. It still seems so unreal to him.

"And January twelfth? If she didn't know she was going to die, then it had to be something else, right?"

"Exactly," Bistro agrees. "Something else happened that

day. Something that made it really clear her running days were over."

"Did Kelley tell you Lindsey was wearing her uniform that day? She dug it out of the equipment room."

"She told me."

"That's odd. Why would she do that?"

"She was making a statement," Bistro says. "Like she wasn't going to be denied."

"Yeah. So, why did she do that on the twelfth?"

"You're starting to think like a cop, Micah." Bistro smiles as if he's pleased. "I'm wondering the same thing, too. Why not the day she found out she was pregnant? Why not January thirteenth, for that matter?"

"You have an answer for that yet?"

"No. I asked your mom—no letters from colleges saying 'No, thanks.' I looked at Lindsey's phone records. There were no calls from colleges. No call from Jonas."

Something happened to his sister that day, something other than dying; but it was just as bad, or so she thought. Micah feels the start of a headache, a tapping against his skull from the inside. He ignores it.

"What about UCLA? Did you ask Kelley about that?"

Bistro nods. "Like I told your mom this morning, Kelley admits UCLA was the only college she thought was good enough for Lindsey. She told me she was in contact with them."

"But Lindsey wouldn't go," Micah repeats.

"Kelley knew that."

"They wouldn't take her without Lindsey. "

"You don't think that's possible?" Bistro counters. "You said yourself that Kelley's been there, done that. She qualified for the Olympics. She competed in Athens."

"So did a lot of athletes," Micah says. "The ones with the

medals are the ones with the top jobs. That's the way it works, in every sport."

"That, or the one *with* the one who's going to medal?"

"Exactly."

Bistro nods. "We're checking into it. Was The Dream everything to Lindsey?" Micah nods. "It meant more to her than Reed did?"

"Much." The room seems somehow brighter. The headaches do that, bleach out color.

"Was Lindsey more into Jonas than Reed?"

Micah pauses. His sister clung to Jonas. For a while, it seemed like Jonas was all she saw. That was so not like her. She even missed a practice once so she could spend time with him, and Kelley got all over her for it. "Yes."

"Which was bigger for your sister—Jonas or The Dream?"

Micah's not so sure anymore. "If she wanted both, she would have found a way for that to happen."

"She was that good?"

"She was that driven."

Bistro nods. He flips a page in his notebook and writes.

"So this gets me off the hook, huh?" Micah asks.

Bistro nods. "Probably."

"What did I say?" Micah asks. "What was important enough for you to write down?"

"Everything you said was important," Bistro says. He waves the notebook. "This can be intimidating to some people."

"To kids."

"Not just kids."

"What did you write down from Kelley today?"

Bistro quotes, "'Lindsey was wearing her track uniform.'"

"Anything else?"

"And you and your sister were arguing."

"She already told you that, before . . ." *Before they found Lindsey.*

"But she remembered more this time."

Micah is all sarcasm. "Yeah, like I told Lindsey she was going to die."

"That's what she says."

Micah catches the doubt in the cop's voice and is relieved. "You don't believe her?"

"Do you?"

Micah shakes his head.

"Sometimes it's the way things are said," Bistro adds. And then: "I don't think you threatened your sister that day, Micah."

"You've changed your mind about me."

Bistro nods. "I don't think you hurt Lindsey. You had no reason to. Not that I can see."

"But Jonas did? Or Reed?"

Bistro won't confirm it. "Let's just say Lindsey being pregnant puts more characters into play."

Micah can only think of two. *Three,* he corrects himself. Kelley had a lot to lose if Lindsey couldn't run anymore. This was Lindsey's senior year. She had scouts from major universities coming to watch her—to watch her and Kelley, too. How they worked together. And scouts from UCLA, of course. Micah doesn't believe for a minute that they would take Kelley without Lindsey. His father was right—his sister and her coach were a package deal. If Lindsey couldn't or wouldn't go to UCLA, the university probably wouldn't hire Kelley. Another failure at the finish line. Micah figures it probably isn't easy going from Olympic athlete to backwoods PE teacher. A chance to coach for a Pac-12 college is a lot more glamorous.

Bistro's next words reel him back in. "I don't think you hurt Lindsey, but I do think you can help her."

"Because I know who killed her."

"Yes." He flips back a few pages in his notebook. "You asked me what I wrote down? Here it is: 'He would have freaked.' Your dad. If he knew Lindsey was seeing Jonas again. If he knew she was pregnant. I think Reed would have freaked, too."

"And Kelley," Micah says.

"Yeah. Your sister was her ticket to the big time."

"Dad wouldn't hurt Lindsey. He loved her."

"I don't doubt it, Micah. But the fact is, children are most often killed by someone who loves them."

"So he's a suspect?"

"He's a person of interest," Bistro agrees.

"He found me there," Micah admits softly. "At the orchard. I was there."

Bistro's face gets that stung look of surprise, but he's quick to react. He flips a few pages and starts writing again.

"Your father told you that?" Micah nods. "What did he say exactly?"

"I was there, running. I remember that part. I remember a lot of running. Toward Lindsey, away from someone—" He shakes his head. "I don't know who, but I was afraid."

"Go deeper, Micah," Bistro urges. "Who was in the orchard with you? Maybe your dad? Was he there?"

"No. He was driving. He almost hit me."

"Do you remember that part? Or did he tell you that?"

"He told me."

"Do you believe it?"

"Yes. It feels right."

"Put yourself in the orchard, Micah," Bistro encourages.

"You see Lindsey. She's running. You turn around—who's there?"

"I'm trying." Micah can hear the tremble in his voice.

"You're scared?"

"Yes. Lindsey is, too. She takes off. Into the trees. I follow her, but she's so fast."

"Then what?"

Micah's inner vision pans from Lindsey's streaking form to the trees behind him. And then his world turns white.

"That's it," he says. He hears the frustration in his voice cutting his words short and sharp. "That's as far as I get."

But Bistro is smiling. "That's a lot more than you had a few days ago," he says.

"Yeah, it is," Micah agrees. And he almost feels like smiling himself.

"You don't remember your dad with you in the orchard? You have any feelings about that?"

"Someone hit me. I remember the swing, the gold watch on his wrist. I think it was my father. I think he did it to calm me down." Or maybe it happened after Dad found Lindsey, when he was pumped up with the horror of it. "I was hysterical."

Bistro is bent over his notebook, scribbling like mad. When he's done, he looks up and offers Micah a fraction of a smile.

"Did your father go into the orchard, Micah? Did he go and look for what spooked you?"

But he can't bring himself to do it, to turn his father over to the police. "Maybe," he says. "It'd make sense."

"And that's it? No other memories?"

"Everything else is white. Except . . . I see Lindsey lying on the ground, patches of snow, leaves in the wind. And I see him in her eyes. I swear I do. The guy who killed her. If I bend closer, if I could just get closer, I'd see him. I'd know." *If it was me.* "What if it *was* me?" he blurts. And he feels an odd calm. Almost as if by confessing his fear to the cop, he was relieved of his guilt.

"I don't think so," Bistro says. "Fear is a complex emotion, Micah. It has a personality. We know when we're afraid of someone else and when we're afraid of ourselves. What does it feel like to you?"

But the clouds still hang low over that area of his mind. He knows he feels caught—but not if he was caught doing something bad, or if he was caught watching someone else do it.

Bistro lays a hand on Micah's shoulder for a moment. "You're looking for the truth," he says. "Not trying to hide from it." And that seems to count for something with him. He heads for the door, but stops before walking through it and turns back. "Your father's talked to you about traumatic memory loss? It's when a person's mind refuses the violent images of someone close to them." He pauses. "It happens when they witness the violence or when they live with—rely on—the perpetrator. Think about that."

12:30 P.M.

Micah tests the door to the boys' locker room. It opens easily. Class is in session—he saw the guys out on the field, knotted into small groups and moving through drills with soccer balls—so the room is silent, except for his footsteps, which echo slightly. He navigates through the maze of tall lockers and past the showers to the bathroom stalls. Sometimes guys hang out in here, the kids who can't throw a ball or who get hopelessly caught in the obstacle course and hurt themselves, but today it's empty. He picks the john farthest from the door, steps in, and slides the lock. The air in the small space is thick. He breathes through his nose, biting into his bottom lip with his teeth.

Pain is the only way you know you're alive. It's the only real way to know it. To believe it.

He bites down until the taste of blood on his tongue makes him gag.

It's not enough.

The cyclone isn't enough; he tried that in class, sitting at his desk with his hand stuffed in his pocket, his fingers pierced more than a pincushion.

He needs more, because the pressure is more. The weight on his chest is crushing.

He pulls his pocketknife out of his sock and drops his pants. His legs are white, covered in thin brown hair. He chooses that soft spot where thigh and hip meet. It's covered up 24/7. No questions, which is good, because he has no answers. He's the kid without a memory.

The first slice carries that sweet burn, like winter. The tension leaves his heart like a pulled ribbon. His chest opens. His lungs expand. Micah tips his head back and closes his eyes.

Lindsey feels nothing now. Nothing. Is that good or bad?

To be alive and feel nothing is bad. It's like living dead.

Slowly suffocating.

When the blood runs over his knee, curls around his calf, Micah opens his eyes and grabs a wad of toilet paper. He stops the flow before it can get to his jeans. Then he captures the wound between two fingers and applies pressure. And lets it flow.

Lindsey pregnant.

Their father. Was Dad so pissed, he killed her?

The blood pools and spills over his fingers.

Kelley lied. Why? What is she hiding? What did she say to Lindsey when she found out his sister was pregnant? What was her reaction when she realized she was twice denied?

Ribbons of bright red blood weave through his fingers and drip to the tile floor.

Kelley didn't get what she wanted, and neither did Dad.

But who lost the most?

He grabs more toilet paper and presses it to the wound he created. He looks at the blade of his knife, smeared with his blood, and his world tilts a little. He knows why he does it, wishes he didn't have to. But he can breathe again, and that's what matters.

Did Kelley kill his sister?

Kelley doesn't do well with defeat. Last season, she argued every point deduction. In Athens, she left the country right after her loss. She didn't stay to cheer on her teammates, she didn't participate in closing ceremonies. The news made a big deal out of it.

So she's a sore loser, he thinks. *Does that make her a killer?*

Micah drops the paper in the toilet and fastens his jeans. He pulls in a deep breath, testing his lungs, and feels only a small pinch. Then he pushes out of the stall and glances at the wall clock: less than fifteen minutes left of the period.

He pauses outside the building. The girls' locker room door stands slightly ajar. Is Kelley in there? Would he find her at the track? In her office, or upstairs in the weight room?

One thing's for sure: He's going to find her.

He moves softly—so softly, he barely feels his feet touch the tarmac—toward the track. A lot of kids are gathered on the green, some spinning and launching shot puts; some tearing through sprints on the far lanes; others practicing with hurdles. He sees the gray head of another PE teacher, Mrs. Martin, before he finds Kelley. She's kneeling beside the rectangular sandpit, measuring long jumps. Her head is down, her dark hair falling forward. The measuring tape snaps back into her hand as she rises.

"You can do better than that, Len." She steps back, and Micah is so close, she almost comes down on his toes. She whirls around and stares into his face. Her cheeks lose color, and she breathes his name before she regains composure.

"What are you doing here, Micah?" Her lips are thin and sharp, like the beak of a bird.

"I want to talk to you."

"You're supposed to be in class."

"Bistro came by," Micah continues. "But you know that. Did you lie to him, too?"

The color returns to her cheeks, but she holds his gaze, long enough that Micah realizes it's a challenge. He doesn't back down.

"So let's talk," she says and pushes past him. "We'll do it over here, Micah, so my students can work on their skills."

She puts a few yards between herself and the scattered groups of kids. Micah follows.

"I didn't lie," she begins.

"You told the vice principal and the nurse that you found me unconscious," he says.

"That's true, Micah."

Micah shakes his head. Everything about her seems calm, rational, composed. Her voice is gentle, caring, and a crock of shit. "You've had a lot of practice. Lying for you is as easy as breathing."

"Micah—"

"We weren't alone," he says. "There were witnesses. But you had me. After that, I was shitting pumpkins. I really thought it was possible I *created* that little talk we had."

Kelley's face changes. She becomes as stiff and still as a statue.

Micah waits. He thinks she's going to explode; possibly internally combust. But she gets it together.

"I'm sorry about that, Micah." But she doesn't regret it— the words are sharp and splintered. "I shouldn't have done that—push you to the point that you fainted. I was too hard on you. But no one was doing anything. Nothing to help you or Lindsey."

"What does that mean?"

"What did Bistro tell you today?" she asks instead.

"The same thing he told you," he counters.

She nods. "Fine. We both know Lindsey was pregnant. I knew it before, of course. Lindsey told me."

First. Before she came to Micah, if she ever did. And maybe that makes sense. He knows nothing about that kind of thing. But telling Kelley would have been hard. It would have been the end of everything. Sudden death for her running, for sure. "How did that make you feel?"

"Furious. I was so angry with her." Her voice trembles a little as she remembers. "She threw her life away. Of course, she didn't see it like that. She thought she could have it all: the baby, the boy, the gold medal. But it doesn't work that way." She's shaking her head vigorously now. "I know. I've been there. She lost everything."

"*You* lost everything," Micah says. "UCLA wouldn't take you without Lindsey, and Lindsey wasn't going. But you kept chipping away at her, thinking you could change her mind." And that easily, it starts making sense to him. "But Lindsey's being pregnant, you couldn't change that."

"UCLA did make me an offer," Kelley admits.

"The offer was for *both* of you."

"I don't know where you're getting your information—"

"They sent Lindsey a letter. UCLA."

Kelley freezes up again. "When?"

"A few weeks ago. She tore it up. That's what Lindsey thought about UCLA and *your* dream."

"She would have gone." Kelley's trying to convince her-self. "London meant more to her than turtles, more than the

Galápagos. It meant more to her than anything else."

"Not anything else." Lindsey felt bad about carving her name into a tree. She would have kept the baby.

"It wasn't too late," Kelley insists. "She would have changed her mind."

"Did you lose it?" Micah wants to know. "You couldn't control her this time. Nothing you said, none of your threats worked, did they?"

"Lindsey was troubled, but she was reasonable."

"Yes, but not you. You don't know how to lose, Coach." And Micah's certainty gains momentum, picks up the beat of his heart, rushes the blood through his veins. "Did you kill her?"

Kelley's face stretches into a silent scream.

When she does speak, her voice is low and harsh.

"I wasn't there," she says, "but you were. No one wants to tell you that. Everyone's so afraid of your 'fragile mental state.' But I know this, Micah Hamilton: You were with Lindsey that afternoon and you were pissed. Add that together."

She takes a step closer to Micah, her face still tight, every feature sharp.

"You bought some of your grades. That's what Lindsey had on you."

Only Lindsey knew about that. And Arthur Bailey, the kid who actually did Micah's chem homework and built the model of thermal transfer for his semester project. Arthur wouldn't tell. He'd be in as much trouble as Micah if he did.

"She was worried about you," Kelley continues, moving closer, crowding him. "She thought you were blowing it *big-time*. And you were, you know. Even a scent of cheating would have the big schools backing off."

But an F on his transcript would eliminate his top pick of universities, too.

"And where would you be without a team, Micah? If no college picked you up?"

Even if Lindsey had talked to Kelley about it, his sister wouldn't have turned him in.

"An arm," Kelley says, her top lip curling back over her teeth. "You'd be lucky to get picked up by some minor league outfit culling for body parts."

"You're lying," Micah protests. *Again. Kelley breathes and it's a lie,* he reminds himself.

But how would she know, otherwise? Lindsey told and she promised she never would.

"Did Lindsey tell your parents? Is that what upset you?"

"She wasn't like that." But his voice is raspy, wavering along with his heart.

"Of course she was." And Kelley laughs. "She was an athlete. Top caliber. And she didn't like to lose."

"You're a world-class liar," Micah says, his voice steady now but his world forever changed, as if it shifted on its axis and Micah is slowly sliding off the face of the earth. "If you believed I cheated, you wouldn't be talking to me—you'd be with the principal and the Commission."

"It's gossip coming from me. Suspicion. Lindsey never told me who was doing the work for you, or even what class it was. But she was ready to. Is that why? Did *you* lose it, Micah, because she told you she was going to turn you in?"

IV

4:55 P.M.

His mother's bedroom door is ajar, and Micah creeps toward it, hoping he doesn't step on a creaking board. Mom doesn't sleep anymore. She lies on the bed, in the shadows, her eyes open and fluid and sometimes stunned, like she's barreling into a car accident.

Micah peeks around the door. She's facing the window. The curtains are open, but it's already growing dark outside, the sky under cloud cover and not yet starred.

He must have made a noise, because she rolls over and gazes at him. She's wearing sweatpants and a sweater and is clutching a wad of damp tissue in her hand.

Bistro was here. She knows about Lindsey. Pregnant. Does she wonder, too, if Dad could have done it? Kill his daughter in a rage?

"Hi," she says. "How was school?"

"Easier today than yesterday," Micah whispers, matching the quiet of the house.

"They say it's like that." She folds her hands over her stomach. "That every day it gets easier."

But she says it without feeling; she doesn't believe it and neither does he, yet.

"Are you hungry?"

"A little." But he knows how to use a microwave. One of the neighbors brought over shopping bags filled with frozen food. Single-serve cartons of lasagna and mac and cheese; some family-size pizzas; Hot Pockets and egg rolls and tiny cheeseburgers. Since his grandfather left, Micah mostly eats alone.

"Do you want me to heat something up for you?"

"No. I'll look in the fridge."

"I'll be out later." Sometimes she does come out and perch on the edge of a dining room chair, not eating, but watching Micah eat.

He decides he needs to move fast. He has to have a plan, one his mother will accept without questioning.

"Vivian is picking me up in a few minutes," he says. "She's going to help me catch up." He has a week's worth of assignments to do.

"Is Vivian helping you?" She's asking about more than homework.

"Yes," Micah says. "It's better when I'm with her." *I'm better.*

"That's good. I'm worried about you, Micah. It's just . . . sometimes I can't do more than that, you know?"

He does know. Some days are harder than others. And today she took another hit. A big one.

"I know." His hand is on the doorknob, and he begins to pull it closed.

"Leave it," she says. "I'll be up."

Micah steps back into the hall. His parents keep the alcohol in a cabinet above the refrigerator. They don't lock it; there's never been a need to.

He finds the step stool, folded and tucked beside the fridge.

He moves aside several dusty boxes of cereal and pulls open the cabinet. Red wine; a variety of makes and models. A bottle of chardonnay his mom uses for cooking—back when she was cooking. Micah takes it from the shelf and stares at the gold label with its curlicues and delicate drawing of leaves. He doubts this will do it—get him the distance he wants—but he pulls the cork and takes a sip anyway.

It tastes like moldy cheese. It doesn't sear his tongue or burn his throat.

It doesn't start a fire in his chest or seep into his veins and pump that novocaine into his system.

It carries no punch at all.

He recorks it and puts it back on the shelf. He won't find tequila. His parents aren't hard drinkers, and he doesn't remember ever seeing them sipping a margarita. Not even when they ate out. He does remember, though, that his grandfather drinks whiskey. A finger of it every night.

He finds it at the very back of the cabinet. Jack Daniel's. Micah recognizes the black label—*like the lettering on a tombstone,* he thinks—before he gets his hand on the bottle. It's half-full. *More than enough,* he thinks. Last time, two shots of tequila in Tommy Anderson's garage was enough.

"Micah?"

He drops the bottle behind a box of Cheerios. He turns, his heart hammering in his throat.

His mother is standing in the arch to the kitchen, her dark hair tousled around her face. "Where's Vivian?"

"She's not here yet."

She nods. "I don't think I ever told her how sorry I am. You know, about her mother."

Vivian's mother died two years ago. More than a year before Micah and Vivian hooked up.

"It's never too late," he says, not thinking.

The words seem to travel over her face, causing a ripple of pain.

"Sorry," Micah adds quickly. "That's not true."

His mom nods again. "There's never enough time. You'll remember that, I think. It will define your moments."

It makes me feel like running, he thinks. *That I have to run or lose it all.*

Did Lindsey feel that way? Is that why she was out on the track her last day?

"Will you tell her for me? Vivian," she prompts. "Tell her I'm sorry."

"Yeah, I'll tell her."

"Thanks." She pulls her hands toward her chest and wavers a moment on her feet. Then she leaves him. He can hear her slippered feet on the wood floor as she walks carefully back to her bedroom.

Micah grabs the bottle of Jack, stashes it behind the blender on the counter, and opens the freezer. His hand falls on a box of chicken-and-broccoli Hot Pockets. He puts one in the microwave for two minutes. Then he takes out the aluminum foil. When it's cooked and wrapped, he grabs his coat off the hook by the back door, stuffs the food into one pocket and the whiskey into the waistband of his jeans. His coat is down and covers the bottle.

But he didn't need to worry. He's out of the house before his mother gets up again or his father comes home.

The wind is sharp, carrying ice in it and whipping around the side of the garage with a scream. He lowers his head and walks into it.

They live on three acres, and behind their house is a swath of wooded hills. In summer, he and Lindsey ran through the trees, up and over the hills, to quicken their reflexes and increase their endurance. In winter, they sometimes came out here with the snowboard; no great challenge, but good practice.

He works on the Hot Pocket as he heads into the woods. Food absorbs alcohol. That means he can drink more of it. He listens to the limbs clack overhead, to the hoot of an owl, and looks for its amber eyes in the darkness.

The snow is less than a foot deep. It's powdery and kicks up as he walks through it. He hopes the clouds move on and the moon shows up. He likes how it turns everything silver. And he wants to find the trees he and Lindsey carved their names into. She chose an alder; Micah chose a birch. They did it years ago, before high school. But the trees will still be there. *Trees live a long life,* he thinks. *Something crazy, like a hundred years.*

He pulls out the Jack Daniel's and uncaps it. He chokes down the first swallow and breathes fire through his nose. *Yeah, this is going to work. Fumes alone probably singed my nose hairs.*

His eyes are watery and he lets them run, swiping at his cheeks as he prepares for another gulp. *Go big,* he tells himself. *More for the money and less kickback.*

He enters the copse of trees, and even though their limbs are bare, it's darker in here. Colder. The wind swirls around his neck and burrows under the collar of his coat. He holds an ungloved hand up in front of his face, and his white skin glows like a lantern. He moves it farther away, watching it dim as the clouds scuttle over the moon and the trees grow thicker around him. Pine and fir mix with maple, alder, and birch. Some trees clothed, some naked.

The thought makes him laugh. His chuckle hits the trees

and bounces back. It sounds eerie. Like he's not alone. Like there are a dozen other guys out here with him, none of them what they seem to be. None of them who people think they are.

Micah, the cheater. No one would believe it. It's not like he's a scholar; mostly Bs with an A or two in the mix. It's enough to get him where he wants to be—USC. The University of Southern California. They have the best baseball program in the country. A bunch of guys went through there before turning pro. And Lindsey would have been there, too.

Cheater. The word is a sneer in his head. He wonders if any of the pros paid for their grades. He heard Rudovich can't read and still earned a college degree.

"I can read!" Micah shouts, and waits for it to hit him on the rebound. He throws back more whiskey.

It's only chemistry. One class. And he needs it. Micah thinks he'll major in PE or sports physiology. Take chemistry in high school and you don't have to repeat it in college. A sweet deal, if you can do it. If all the symbols didn't read like a foreign language. If he could only understand action and reaction.

He pulls from the bottle again and could swear, for a moment, that flames are shooting out of his mouth. Then he feels it flush down his esophagus, burn through each branch and pocket of his lungs, and finally pool in his stomach. The numbness begins. First his toes and fingers—the cold sting ebbs. Pins and needles set in. He still feels the rough material of his jeans against his knees as he trudges through the snow. He feels the T-shirt he's wearing inch up under his coat and the palm print of the wind against his exposed skin, but it's a good thing now. His body is suddenly roasting.

Yes. This is how he remembers it. The buzz, the warmth. And soon the not caring.

He stumbles and reaches out, resting his hands against the bark of an alder tree. He peers closely at its surface. *Nope, not this one.* Lindsey used his pocketknife to carve her name, before she started caring more about living things and less about her own mortality.

It was a group of trees that went birch, birch, maple, alder. That's how they remembered it, how they were able to come back months, even a year later when they wanted to see their names etched in the wood.

Lindsey's was long enough, it almost wrapped around the trunk of the tree. Months after she carved it, she added the petals of a flower so that the circle was complete.

Micah stops at the next alder, runs his hands over the surface, but it's too smooth. And it's too dark now to really tell the trees apart. Finding *Lindsey Michelle Hamilton* would be like looking for a rose under the fields of snow that stretch out around him. In early spring, flowers often bloom, a splotch of red or yellow against the vast whiteness, and they're easy to find. But it's the middle of January and it's dark, and everything is dead.

Micah trips and falls forward. He stretches his arm out, lifting the bottle above his body as he hits the ground. It's a soft landing that sprays powder into the air. He rolls over. The sky is ringed by the bony, gnarled limbs of the trees. The moon half hides in the clouds. A few stars burn steadily.

Are you up, there, Lindsey? Did I do that to you? Did Dad?

Lindsey's eyes in his dream were wide in her pale face, the image of a man staring out. He tries to peer closer at them. Who is that? *Who was the last person you laid eyes on? Who killed you, Lindsey?*

The dream *feels* like reality. And maybe it is. Another

memory Micah swaddled in cotton because he's too afraid to look at it.

"Bring it on!" he shouts. He can take it. He can take anything now.

Even if it's me? Even if looking into Lindsey's eyes is like looking into a mirror?

His stomach heaves.

No, it's not. It's not me.

He staggers to his feet and takes another swig from the bottle. The flare of a rocket, that's what it feels like going down. But this time it reaches his fingers and toes. No more pins and needles. Now he's all liquid, no bone. He feels like a water balloon in the snow, slipping, sliding, tumbling downhill.

V

7:30 P.M.

Micah doesn't fall asleep but into a trance. He stares into the darkness, the bushy tops of the fir trees swaying against a sky studded with stars. Clouds drift, baring the moon and making the hills look like the foamy crests of waves.

His first coherent thought is: *Wow, I really must have fallen down the slope.* He left the copse of birch and alder for the fir trees at the bottom. The mountains aren't steep here, but they're long. He doesn't feel cold, though the snow must have melted through his jeans, slipped under his coat.

He still has a buzz going. In fact, he can actually hear it, the rush of blood inside his head.

The sound captured in seashells, he thinks.

Maybe someone will come along, pick me up, and hold me to their ear. The thought makes him laugh. It gurgles in his throat and then scratches against the sky.

He lifts his arms and tries to gather clouds, but like sand, they drift between his fingers.

Weird. The whole world is out of control. As weird as Lindsey pregnant.

Who's the father? Reed or Jonas?

Jonas, Micah decides. She was so into him.

Did Jonas freak when he found out he was going to be a father?

Did Reed freak when Lindsey let him have it—*Sorry, dude, but the baby isn't yours*?

Did Dad freak when he found out his gifted daughter was never going to do all the things everyone thought she would?

Did Kelley freak when she realized she held a ticket to a show that was canceled?

Did Micah freak?

A phone rings. It peals into the rolling silence of the landscape. It rings twice before he realizes it's his phone—his mom's, really.

He rummages through his pockets, but by the time he finds the phone, the call has gone to voicemail. On the screen, there's a picture of a single calla lily, snow landing on its open petals.

Lindsey's flower. Her favorite, the ones that covered her coffin. His mother plucked several from the arrangement before they left the graveside. One is pressed between glass and hanging above their mother's nightstand.

Vivian's number is displayed over the picture of the lily. He missed her. *Misses* her.

Damn. He wanted to answer that.

The alcohol delays his reflexes. A full minute later he realizes that he can call her back. He laughs—*You're an ass, Hamilton*—and hits speed dial.

"Where are you?" she asks.

"Well, hello, baby," Micah says. "Good evening to you, too."

He waits for Vivian to say something, but it takes her a moment. "What are you doing?" Her voice is hesitant, wary even.

"Looking at the stars."

"Really?"

"You doubt me?" he says, laughter filling his mouth, slurring his words.

"Where are you?" she asks again.

"Home."

"You're not home," Vivian retorts. "I'm here, standing on your front porch, and you are not here, Micah."

"I'm in the backyard." He laughs. "Way back of the backyard."

"You're not making sense."

"Nothing makes sense, Viv. Sometimes you just gotta join the crowd."

"Are you drinking?"

The last time—the one and only other time—Micah drank, he called her on the phone and sang "Bleeding Love" to her.

"I understand your worry," he says. "But I don't have it in me tonight. No song in my heart."

"Where are you, Micah?"

"In the way back of the way back. Lying in the snow and looking for Lindsey."

"I'm coming," she says.

"I'll wait for you."

A moment later she says, "Damn, it's dark back here." Her breath is thicker. Small gasps. She really is coming for him.

"I'm down the slope. Through the trees and down the slope. Be careful, though," he warns, "it's a long drop."

"Are you hurt, Micah?"

He thinks about that. "My heart's on fire."

"Yeah," she agrees quietly. Her voice is a little breathless as she stomps through the snow. "I don't know if it gets better or if you just get used to it."

"I don't want to get used to it."

"I'm in the trees now," Vivian says.

"I couldn't find Lindsey there. It was too dark."

"I'll help you. Sometimes they hide," she confides. "Sometimes they're buried. Have you noticed? The human heart is deep. It took me months to find my mother after she died."

Micah contemplates that. "I don't like the sound of that, Viv," he says. "I'm missing her now."

"That's the real bitch. But it's a process. You have to grieve first." Then she announces, "I found the slope." Her voice rises at the end. "Lost my footing. Where are you, Micah? Stand up. Wave your arms. Call out to me."

Micah stirs but falls back against the snow when his head does a three-sixty. "Whoa! I have *The Exorcist* going on here."

"I have a flashlight," Vivian says. "I'm about halfway down the hill, but I don't see you."

He lifts his arms and waves them, but they're too heavy to keep in the air for long. "Vivian," he bellows, doing his best to sound like Stanley in *A Streetcar Named Desire*. The Drama Club did the play last year, when Lindsey was president. She painted scenery and worked the lights.

"I can hear you," Vivian says.

Micah sees the sweeping beam of her flashlight.

"Over here," he calls, but then his voice becomes heavy and the effort too much. "Your light is here."

"I see you," Vivian says. "I'm hanging up, Micah."

He hears the crunch of her boots in the snow, and a moment later Micah's world goes from cold to hot, from darkness to light. She looks down at him and the moon shimmers over her face, making her look . . . cosmic. If Micah ever discovers a star, he'll name it Vivian.

"I'm drunk," he says.

"Definitely." She pulls at the hem of her parka, holding it over the seat of her pants before she kind of folds herself down beside him.

"That was pretty. Really graceful." Vivian's always had that: grace. The way her body moves reminds him of water flowing easily over the stones in a river. "I wouldn't mind being the rocks your river flows over."

Vivian snorts.

"I think I'm a poet," he protests.

"You're drinking like one," she agrees.

"I've missed you."

"I'm here now." She finds his hand in the snow and wraps hers around it. "You're cold."

"I miss Lindsey."

"I know."

"I'm just going to keep on missing her, aren't I?"

Vivian nods. "That's about it."

Micah looks up at the stars, but tightens his hand around Vivian's. "'Her feet are wings of solid gold that lift her above the slow sparrows.' I wrote that for Lindsey. She pinned it to her wall." It's still there.

"Really?" Surprise makes her voice float. "You *are* a poet."

"I've written a few."

"I've never seen them."

"I was a tween nerd at the time. I wrote some songs, too, though. They were good. I wanted to be Justin Timberlake." He laughs. "I even got Lindsey to sing backup for me a couple of times."

Vivian chuckles. "I would have loved to see that."

"I strummed my guitar—I only ever learned two chords—

and we sang like we actually had a chance. Mom and Dad sat on buckets in the garage, these huge grins eating up their faces. They loved stupid stuff like that."

"It wasn't stupid."

"And Lindsey shook these maracas we picked up in Costa Rica one summer. I love that sound—like rain on the roof. Lindsey shook those and then, when the chorus came up, she held one in front of her like it was a microphone and belted out the words like they were worth it."

He's crying. He doesn't feel the tears on his face, but his nose and throat are full of mucus and his voice disappears entirely in a knot of sobs.

He feels Vivian beside him, full length. She must have lain down. And now her arm is slung over his chest, her hand is stroking his face, tangling in his hair. He feels her lips on his forehead, her breath against his ear, his face in the warm curve of her neck.

He didn't find Lindsey. The booze wasn't good for that, or anything else, really. It's Vivian who softens the sharp edges of reality.

Micah listens to his breathing. Gradually it calms until all he hears is a quiet rasp.

"Sorry," he mumbles.

"What? Boys don't cry? That's bullshit," Vivian declares.

"I was talking about the booze." But he was worried more about the crying.

"I expected something like this. When my mom died, I started smoking my father's cigarettes."

"It doesn't help," Micah says.

"No. It's stupid."

"Are you pissed?"

"No. It's part of the experience. I was mad for a while and

I wanted to stay that way. I knew as soon as I let go of that, I'd drown. Too much sadness waiting for me." She starts to float away from him, but catches herself and says, "You're trying to cope."

"I'm failing."

"You're just starting. It's a long process."

"I don't know if I'll ever accept it. Especially if I could have done something to stop it. Or if I was the one who did it."

He feels her whole body go from welcome to freeze zone in a microsecond. "You didn't, Micah—"

"No, I don't think so, but there's evidence."

"What evidence?"

"I was there."

"Says your father."

"But it's true. I remember enough, I'm sure I was there. And one more thing." He sighs heavily, and his hand on the neck of the Jack Daniel's tightens. "Arthur was doing more than tutoring me," he confesses. "He did most of my homework—"

"He tutored you through most of your homework," she corrects.

"No. I never understood it. Not really. I was sinking. Fast. I paid Arthur double for the homework and a whopping two hundred dollars for my semester project." Which is due in a couple of weeks, and Micah wonders if he'll turn it in. He doesn't think so.

He watches Vivian's face adjust to the fact that her boyfriend is a cheater.

"I'm sorry, Viv." His gut twists, and he feels the distance build between them. "It's the only time I've ever done anything like that. I couldn't fail it again, you know?"

"Not if you want USC."

"Exactly." They slip into silence for a moment. "Am I *tin cũ*?" Old news.

Vivian's hand moves across his chest, and she taps her fingers over his heart. "You tried, Micah. I know that for sure. I spent a lot of time waiting for you to finish up with Arthur. I *heard* you trying."

"It shouldn't have mattered so much."

"But chem is a requirement for graduation. And not everyone is good at it." Her lips purse. "It would be like making Matt Baylor take PE." Baylor is a danger to himself when it comes to anything that bounces or rolls. "But PE isn't required."

"And he plays a mean trumpet."

"Yeah. So why don't they have another option for chem?"

"I like your thinking," Micah says, his insides loosening.

"It's true. If you're no good at PE, you take band or cheer and you're still college-bound. You're no good at chem, and what? You can flip burgers at Jack in the Box?"

Micah feels a grin spread across his face. They're okay. And he loves when Vivian goes off on a tangent. But the fierce cast to her face softens to confusion as he watches.

"What does your cheating have to do with Lindsey?"

"Motive," he says. "She knew. And she told Kelley. Maybe she would have gone to the Commission about it, too."

"And ruin your chances for a baseball scholarship? That never would have happened. Lindsey wouldn't have told. She wasn't like that."

"That's what I said."

"But Kelley thinks Lindsey was going to do it?"

"According to her, Linds wasn't going to go down alone."

Vivian's face goes blank. "What does that mean?"

And so he tells her about Lindsey's being pregnant and Bistro's short list of suspects.

"Jonas Moore." Vivian shakes her head. "I thought they were over. Long over. Wham, bam, thank you, ma'am." Micah winces. "Sorry. But he didn't treat her very well. They were hot and heavy one day. The next, he was Siberia and she was still baking on a beach in Tahiti."

Micah lets this sink in. He knew his sister was into Jonas; he didn't know it ended abruptly. That Lindsey was simply cut loose.

"In a way, it wasn't even personal," she adds. "Jonas and all those leatherheads, they don't stick too long with one girl. Ever."

"I thought Lindsey was okay with the breakup."

Vivian shakes her head. "She was *so* into him. Remember that Sharpie tattoo?"

He didn't, not until now. Jonas's playing number—75—and Lindsey's then-fastest run time—four minutes, nineteen seconds—in a fancy scroll on her upper arm, in blue and gold. Merwin's school colors. She'd had it done in the spring.

"She wasn't okay. Not at first. Which is a totally healthy reaction," she assures him. But then she goes on. "She followed him around for a few days afterward. The guys—Jonas's friends—I heard them call her—" She pauses and her face twists.

"What?"

"Mutt."

Micah's breath thins and sadness flutters in his throat. "I didn't know that."

"It was only for a week, maybe not even that long. Lindsey got over it pretty fast. Faster than I would have. . . ."

"Why didn't I hear about it?"

"You were in the playoffs, and then you had that weekend at Mariners camp. It blew over fast. Like I said, Lindsey got it together. She was reasonable. She had running to fall back on. A couple of weeks later, she shaved a little time off her run and scrubbed the numbers off her arm. Pretty in-your-face, huh?"

"Yeah."

"I wonder what Jonas said about being a daddy. That would have thrown a serious wrench into his NFL dream."

"Do you think Lindsey told him?"

Vivian thinks about that. "Maybe not. I don't think I'd run to him, after the way he treated her last year."

Micah doesn't mention that Lindsey might have seen Jonas in the fall. Maybe even over Christmas. He lets her figure it out on her own.

"She didn't look pregnant to me," Vivian says. "Not at all. I mean, it is winter and all, and she was probably bundled up a lot, but I didn't notice it even a little."

Neither did Micah.

"Oh," she says, her eyes rounding. "She wasn't that far along."

"Bistro said almost four months."

"She's been seeing Jonas?" Vivian's voice rises with her surprise. "This year?"

"Bistro thinks so."

"Did your father know?"

"Probably."

"Who else knew?"

"Jonas, and Kelley." Micah can't shake her loose. She had plenty of motive, even if it was a man's face he saw in his sister's eyes.

"Jonas? I doubt it. He was pretty good at keeping himself the center of his universe." Her forehead scrunches up. "Your dad; I thought that was possible. Any time you lie you have a reason for it, you know? But Kelley, she had the most to lose."

"Another chance at the Olympics."

Vivian agrees. "But Bistro doesn't think so?"

"Statistics. Most kids, when they're murdered, it's a family member."

"Or the boyfriend. That happens often enough. And Reed, he was . . . obsessed. I mean, talk about casting a shadow."

"What does that mean?"

"He followed her everywhere. He waited for her outside her classes, sat in the bleachers when she was doing sprints." Vivian shakes her head.

"She never complained about it."

Vivian shrugs. "She tried to cut him loose. She wasn't good at that kind of thing, I think. She was gentle, like you. Which is another reason why I know you could never hurt her. Not for any reason."

"Yeah. But Bistro had me at the top of his list." Until they found out Lindsey was pregnant.

He feels her turn toward him, her nose brushing his chin. "How do you know that? For sure?"

"He acted like it," Micah says. "And anyway, I was there. I just wish I could remember more. I have flashes of memory. Pieces . . . I remember running after her, and watching her fade into the trees. I remember standing in the middle of the road—Twin Ferry Road—in front of the orchard, screaming at my father. It's weird. I see it like a movie—I'm watching myself do it. But it's real. It happened."

"You remember the before and the after?"

Micah nods. "Yeah. I think so. I'm crying and screaming.

I'm hysterical, and my father isn't much better."

"What were you saying?"

But his memory has always been mute. Until now. As Micah pushes himself backward, sound comes crashing into the present.

"'She's dead. She's dead.' Over and over." And as he watches it unfold inside his head again, more pieces float into place. He lifts a hand and rubs his face. "My father hit me. I remember that. He was yelling at me to shut up, but I couldn't, and then he hit me."

Clouds shift, cover the moon, and deepen the shadows around them. His hand on hers tightens. "I knew she was dead."

VI

8:00 P.M.

They walk through the snow, Vivian beside him but not touching. Sometimes their arms brush and the nylon of their jackets whispers. He feels the cold now as a slow burn from his toes and fingertips. Vivian's teeth chatter, and he wants to reach out and pull her close, warm her, but is afraid she doesn't want him, doesn't trust him now.

They're close enough to the house now that he can see his parents in the kitchen, his father walking past the window. The temperature continues its descent, and a sheet of snow breaks loose and slips off the roof.

"My father thought it was me."

"But he doesn't anymore?"

"I freaked on him." Micah tells her about this morning. "He shouldn't have believed it. I mean, I've never done anything to Lindsey before, or to anyone else. Ever."

"My marshmallow," Vivian murmurs.

"Yeah." The endearment is growing on him. "Now my father thinks it's Jonas. I guess Bistro will check that out."

"Yeah, let the police figure it out," she says, and reaches for his hand.

"But I knew. *I knew she was dead.*" At first as a feeling, and now with memory.

"You didn't kill her, Micah. I could never believe that. You loved her, like I love Minh."

Minh was Vivian's rock when their mother died. He's away at college now, but sends her silly postcards with commentary from the trenches of dorm life.

Micah doesn't go to school the next morning, not right away. He asks Vivian to drop him off at the police station.

"Why?"

"I want to talk to Bistro."

"Are you going to tell him what you remember?"

"He already knows." *Some of it.*

Vivian pulls up outside the tan brick building. "Do you want me to wait for you?"

He shakes his head. "Maybe he'll drop me off." If not, it's a short walk. Hood Valley is a small town.

Micah has never been inside a police station before. The glass doors open into a small room lined with plastic chairs. The walls are brown paneling, and the old tile on the floor is worn to the color of putty. Something like a window is carved out in the wall in front of him. It's made of Plexiglas, and there's an orange button: RING FOR ASSISTANCE. Beside that is a metal door painted a deep shade of brown to blend in with the 1980s décor.

The only other people in the room at this hour are an elderly couple huddled over a clipboard of papers.

It's a few minutes before someone answers his buzz.

"Can I help you?" She's dressed in a khaki uniform and has a radio attached to her shoulder.

Micah steps closer to the window. "Yes," he says. "Is Bistro here?"

The woman's eyebrows shoot up. "That's *Detective* Bistro," she reprimands. "I don't suppose he's expecting you?"

"Sorry," he says.

"And who may I say is calling?"

"Micah Hamilton."

Her eyes change; the irritation seems to snap out of them. "Yeah, he's here. Just got in, so it could be a minute. You want to sit down while I get him?"

She disappears behind the paneling. Micah doesn't want to sit. He pivots on his heels and looks at the posters. There are a few that show what happens to YOU ON DRUGS. Another has a few kids on it, standing in a shadowy street, only their faces, eyes wide with fear, visible; RUN THIS WAY, and a picture of St. Thomas's Shelter.

He walks toward the other side of the room and a flank of posters that turn out to be America's Most Wanted. Many are mug shots, but a few look more like what you'd find in a family photo album. America's Top Twenty. Sixteen men; four women. He wonders: *Does that mean twenty percent of criminals are female?*

"Micah?" Bistro is surprised by his visit. His voice shows it, but so does his face, which is wide open.

"I thought I could talk to you for a minute."

"Sure." He holds the door open. "You an early riser?"

"I am now."

Bistro nods, like he knows all about sleepless nights.

His office is a desk pushed up against another desk in a big room that includes a copier, a slotted wall for mail, and more posters of crimes and criminals.

"Sit down, Micah." Bistro waves at a chair. "You want coffee?"

"No, thanks." He sits. "I think Kelley saw me waiting for Lindsey, outside the auditorium."

"That makes sense," Bistro says, and sits down himself, so close their knees almost touch. "We know how you probably got those handprints on your T-shirt."

"Yeah."

"Lindsey's friends say she was agitated, in a hurry. She wiped her hands some on a towel and hustled out of there."

"And I was waiting."

Bistro nods. "You worked out at the batting cages," he adds. "You signed in. You hit five hundred balls. That took forty minutes."

"I didn't know that." But it feels right. He always hits the cages starting in January.

"Your father doesn't want us helping your memory along," Bistro explains, "but I don't suppose that'll hurt any."

"I want to know."

"I figure you were pretty heated, left the cages carrying your sweatshirt. Maybe you tried to talk to your sister after getting her text. The way her hand printed on your shirt, it looks to me like maybe she didn't want to talk to you just then."

"She pushed me away," Micah says, and it feels so true, he rummages around inside his head for a matching memory. For a few flashes of a scene. But it doesn't materialize. "Maybe."

"Sounds reasonable." Bistro pulls a folder across the desk and opens it. "You know what was in that text Lindsey sent you?"

"You found her phone?"

"No. We found yours. You lost it when you were running, we figure. Lindsey lost hers then, too. Yours we found in the orchard. It was in sorry condition, but our lab was able to get it up and running." He places his finger on a piece of paper and runs it along some typed words. "Here it is. Lindsey's own words: 'Sorry. I would never tell. Ever. I'm just really messed up right now, you know?'"

Micah sits back. His breath catches in his throat, and he releases it. "That's it?"

"Yeah." Bistro closes the folder and pins Micah with his eyes. "You don't seem too concerned about it."

He isn't. It just confirms what he's always known: Lindsey wouldn't have ratted on him.

"I'd be concerned, Micah. What wasn't she going to tell?"

Micah stares at him, his mouth dry, his tongue thick. His blood passes through his ears with the roar of a roller coaster. He feels for the cyclone in his jeans pocket. The points poke against the material and he strokes them, wanting to get closer, wanting to cut.

"Come on. You've been honest all along, haven't you?" But Bistro's tone is clipped, doubting. "What's your secret, Micah?"

"I cheated," Micah admits.

Bistro picks up a pencil but doesn't use it. "And Lindsey knew?"

"Yes."

"She was going to tell?"

"Kelley says so."

"And your sister told you so, too."

"I don't remember that conversation. And I don't believe it."

"It happened." Bistro taps the folder. "I love when the dead speak for themselves. It doesn't happen very often, but when it does, you can't argue with it."

"Maybe she said it. But she wouldn't have done it."

"What did you cheat on? Your girlfriend? A test?"

"Chemistry," Micah confesses. "Every homework assignment. A take-home quiz. My final project."

Bistro sits back, tapping his pencil against the desk. He's frowning as he tries to work this piece of information into the equation of Lindsey's murder.

"What would that do to an athlete like you?"

Micah shrugs. "I don't know." But he does. It would kill The Dream, same as Lindsey's pregnancy knocked her out of the Olympics.

"You wouldn't play this year."

"Probably not."

"So it would be the end."

"I'd have next year."

"Maybe. But what college would pick you up?"

"Jeter didn't go to college," Micah says. "A lot of guys didn't."

"But you're not Jeter."

"You think I killed Lindsey." *To cover up my chem grade.*

"We're back to that," Bistro agrees. "You're a suspect."

Micah shakes his head. "It wasn't me."

Bistro takes a sip of coffee, then places the mug carefully on the blotter on his desk. "Lindsey wasn't going down alone."

"You sound like Kelley."

"She knew your sister well."

Micah has nothing to say to that. Kelley did know Lindsey, better than their parents did. Probably better than Micah did. "We know you were in the orchard. For sure. We have physical evidence that places you at the scene."

"My father was telling the truth." Bistro nods. "Was it my shoes?"

Now the detective shakes his head. "They didn't tell us much. There were similarities in the soil samples, but that only means you were there at some point. Could have been days before Lindsey was killed. No, we know you were there,

Micah, because we took castings of all the hand- and footprints in the earth around your sister.

"We have prints from Lindsey's shoes, of course. Several others, too—the orchard is really popular with kids your age. A lot of you go in there to smoke, drink . . . One of those prints was a definite match to your Nikes. The print of another shoe probably belongs to your father. We have a warrant now. An officer is on his way to your house. He'll collect your father's shoes."

Bistro leans forward, tension bunching his shoulders.

"But you know what I find really interesting, Micah? There was only one set of handprints. A left print at Lindsey's shoulder; a right print near her opposite elbow. Knees in the earth beside her hip. Someone stopped, bent over her. There's evidence she was moved a little, so maybe you picked her up, held her. Those handprints—they were yours, Micah. We matched them to prints we lifted from your textbooks, which we found inside your locker. We had a warrant to go in there."

"I was there when Lindsey died." *But I already knew this.* "What does that mean? Why did I pick her up?"

"I can't tell you for sure—only you can do that." Then he pauses, and says: "Did you know, Micah, that we can figure out how much a man weighs from the shoe impressions he makes in the dirt?" He smiles. "Science is beautiful." Bistro sits back. "So we're pretty sure we have your dad in the orchard, too."

"He didn't kill her."

"You keep saying that, but unless you have evidence to add to it, we're down to two possibilities." Bistro pauses, but Micah refuses to fill the silence. "No confession?" Another pause, more silence. Then: "That's okay. The truth is, your father is what we call an obvious pick. Statistics point the finger that way, but there are other inconsistencies—his refusal to turn over his shoes, his inability to account clearly for his time that afternoon, his being in the orchard and not mentioning it . . . Makes people like me real suspicious."

"What about Kelley?" Micah asks. "Any shoe prints that could have been hers?"

"I know you like her for this."

"She's a liar." He tells about the track and how she told the vice principal she found him unconscious.

"People lie for a lot of reasons. She felt bad about pushing you. I understand that." He leans forward and drops the pen on the desk. "Your father asked us not to put pressure on you, Micah."

Micah tells him about UCLA. Kelley practically admitted the offer was for both of them.

Bistro hesitates, but his eyes don't waver. "We know," he says. "And you're right. They weren't going to take Kelley. Not without your sister."

"She told you that?"

"Not at first. We had to dig a little, but yeah, she was in conversation with the university. And she seems to think Lindsey was her ticket. She all but promised her to UCLA." Kelley was going to get her way, no matter what.

"She can't." His voice is little more than a whisper. Apparently, Kelley can do anything.

"But she did. I think your sister knew it, and that was the reason why she wouldn't take Kelley's calls. But I also think Lindsey would have gone with her. Everyone I talk to says it: An athlete is about as good as her coach. Lindsey was afraid of going it without Kelley."

Micah believes it, too. "But Lindsey was pregnant."

"True, but lots of women have babies and go on to com-

pete at the Olympic level. It wasn't convenient," Bistro continues, "the situation wasn't optimal, but it wasn't the end of
the world, either."

It was for Lindsey.

"But Kelley lied about UCLA."

"It doesn't make her look good," Bistro agrees.

"She lied about a lot of things. She had the most to lose,
and everyone knows Kelley is a sore loser."

"She wasn't in the orchard, Micah. There's no evidence
she was ever there."

"You took her shoes, too."

"Every pair. Her memory is questionable, no doubt about
it. And she could have cooperated with us more. But evidence
doesn't lie." Bistro lifts a folder from the desk and holds it up.
"The last of the scene was processed. Kelley isn't anywhere
in there."

SUNDAY, JANUARY 23

I

4:40 P.M.

Micah is in the Nguyens' garage, tinkering with the radio. He meant to get here sooner, a day or two ago, but he loses track of time, not realizing its passage until the sky is almost dark. And then it's too late.

"Hey, my father says you earned a place at the table tonight."

Micah lifts his head and gazes at Vivian. Snow is melting in her hair and on the sleeves of her blue sweater. She ran out of the house without her coat.

"If you were pregnant, who would you tell?"

The question catches her off guard—he expected it to—but only for a moment.

"Minh," she responds easily.

"Who's the last person?"

Her frown deepens. "My father, probably."

Micah lays the screwdriver on the workbench, then crosses his arms and stares up at the garage ceiling. Mr. Nguyen is old-school in some ways. Nine dried chicken carcasses hang from the exposed rafters. Vivian says they're to ward off spirit hunters. In Vietnam, nine is a lucky number.

"My sister didn't tell me," Micah says.

He feels Vivian approach him. Her shadow falls across his chest, and then her fingers land softly on his arm.

"I don't think she wanted to face it," she says. "It would put everything on hold. It's hard going from fast-forward to pause."

"We were close. We talked." But not about everything. Lindsey never spoke to him about Jonas, not when they were dating and not after they broke up.

"She wrote you that note," she reminds him. "I think she was trying to tell you."

"Remember that dream I told you about, the one with Lindsey lying in the snow? She's dead already and curled up on her side, and maybe she tried to fight back—her hands are fists. Her eyes are open and I can see him, reflected there. The guy who killed her. Only it's like looking in a mirror at a fun house, you know? The image is distorted, his face stretched out. So I don't recognize him. Not really. At least my mind doesn't, but something inside me does. . . ."

He realizes he's falling backward into memory. His voice is growing distant, and Vivian's fingers contract in his sweater.

"Who is it?"

He leans against the workbench and gazes at her face. Soft. Everything about Vivian is ready to believe. Since Lindsey died, most people stare at him with a "convince me" attitude. But not Viv; she's as open, as clean as rain. He feels himself cringe on the inside, because what he's going to say next will be do or die for them.

"It's me, or it's my father. That's what Bistro thinks."

He watches her pulse beat at the base of her throat.

"He told you that?"

"Friday morning."

"He's sure? He has evidence and everything?"

Micah nods. "He's always had evidence that I was there."

She lifts her hands, twists them in front of her, weaving her fingers together to try to control her nerves.

"You're scared," he says quietly.

"You're starting to scare me," she admits.

"You know more than anyone else. You should be scared. You could be looking at a murderer. You could be in love with a killer."

Her face pales, but she shakes her head. "No. I told you, I don't believe it."

"Some people, some things, are a lost cause."

"Not you." Her voice holds steady.

"Why are you so sure?"

She leans in, so close that he can smell the peaches in her hair. "Every time I even *start* to doubt you, I remember every time I saw you and Lindsey together. You loved each other, even when you were arguing. Even when you were trying to outdo each other." Her voice is full of passion. "It's someone else. If not Kelley"—she takes a deep breath—"then maybe it *was* your father. Maybe Bistro is right about that. Or maybe it was Reed. The guy looks like Clark Kent on the outside, but he has a serious edge."

"Why do you say that?"

"He took Belinda Maize to the winter formal last year and drove her out way past the reservoir and left her there."

Micah remembers hearing something about that, but it sounded too out-there to be true. He teased Reed about it, and the guy had turned purple before he caught a breath and denied it.

"He took her cell phone, too, so she couldn't call her folks. And you know why?" Viv lifts her face defiantly. "She called him cheap. That's it."

"That really happened?"

"Belinda's parents reported it to the police. Bistro should know about that."

"But they took his shoes. They must have been clean." Because Reed is still walking around on the outside. Bistro's dismissed him as a suspect.

"So maybe he trashed the ones he was wearing," Vivian says. "He loses his cool fast. Isn't that what the cops are looking for?"

"He told me he was glad Lindsey was dead." He hears Vivian gasp, and he tells her about their fight in the boys' bathroom. "Tynes broke it up, and I haven't seen Reed since."

"Maybe they arrested him."

"I don't know. The police were at my house Friday morning. They took my father's shoes."

She considers that, the cast of her face serious, and then says, "Good. Because then you'll know, one way or the other."

"What if it *is* my dad I see in Lindsey's eyes?" The image his instincts seem to recognize? The dream is the only vivid picture Micah has of his sister's death—what if it's talking to him? What if what he knows, what he's buried, is trying to find a way out? Any way out? "What if it's me? Really, Viv. You keep saying no, but what if?"

"You said it was a dream."

"It doesn't feel like a dream anymore."

"Your gut never lies—" she begins.

"Exactly."

"So why don't you try it on? Give yourself one full minute with it."

"Say to myself, 'I killed Lindsey,' and try to believe it?"

Mrs. Eisenberg says this when she wants them to write a short story or a character sketch.

"You have to believe in order for us to."

And so Micah closes his eyes and holds on to the thought. He tries to picture it: him chasing Lindsey like he remembers; catching her, which seems impossible; choking her—but he can't get his hands around her throat. He tries to picture launching himself at her, knocking her down—but it's not possible. Not even when he considers her threats to expose him. To ruin him.

Not even when he takes baseball forever out of his life.

He opens his eyes and finds Vivian watching him.

"It's not you, is it?" Her voice is full of confidence.

"No." His smile doesn't last long, though. "But, you know, I tried this last night—with my dad, not me—and I came up empty."

"What do you get when you make Kelley the killer?"

He gets light on his feet. His heart freezes between beats. And fear crawls over his shoulders and wraps around his throat.

Vivian can tell from his face. "It's her." And she doesn't care what Bistro or the evidence says.

Micah looks at the clock on the Mini's dash as they pull into the driveway. Eight thirty. He ate dinner with Vivian and her father, hung around afterward and listened to *The Diamond Report* on the radio with Mr. Nguyen. They talked about the Mariners, the new rule on shutouts, and whether or not Derek Jeter would get married this year. On the way to the door, Mr. Nguyen took one of Micah's hands and placed a polished stone the color of jade into it.

"We are very sorry here about your sister," he said. "This is a *bùa*. I carry one, too, ever since Vivian's mother passed. It will draw the good spirits close."

Micah stroked the rock with his thumb. It was cold, smooth. "Thanks, Mr. Nguyen. I'll hold on to it."

"That's a good idea," he said, and Micah walked out into the icy night air.

"The police are here," Vivian says, snapping Micah into the present.

A patrol car is parked in the driveway. Its interior is dark. Next to it, his father's Acadia is parked at an angle, steam rising from the cooling engine.

"Great."

"You want me to drive around for a while?" Vivian offers.

But he shakes his head. "I want to know." Then he leans over the console and kisses her. He'll never get used to how soft she is, how small and perfect.

"I'll pick you up in the morning?"

"Yeah." *Unless they're here to arrest me.*

He stands on the front porch and watches her reverse out and drive south—away from him, from the scene he's about to walk into, toward school and home.

His parents are in the kitchen. Bistro is there, too. They each have a full cup of coffee.

"Hi, Micah," the detective says. "You want to join us?"

What for? he wonders. *Did they figure it out? Or did they toss a coin? Who's leaving tonight in handcuffs—me or Dad?*

His mom pulls out the chair next to hers. "Come sit, Micah. The police have some questions."

"We'll answer the questions," his father says. "Your mother and I."

Bistro nods. "My questions are for you, Dr. Hamilton," he says, then looks at Micah. "But if you have anything to add, Micah—a different perspective, maybe—I want you to let me know."

Micah sits down. He shrugs out of his coat and lets it drape over the back of his chair. Bistro is across the table, his father to his left. They're both watching him, and he becomes aware of his hands—they're slick, shaking, and he's rubbing them over his thighs. He tucks them under his legs.

"January twelfth," Bistro says and flips a few pages in his notebook. "You gave us an account of your day, Mr. Hamilton." *The day Lindsey died.* "It doesn't match up with some of the details we've gathered."

"What details?" his father demands. His voice is sharp. "Name them."

"Your receptionist and a man with an office downstairs from yours both reported your leaving at one thirty."

"Lunch," his father says.

"You didn't come back."

His father hesitates. His lips form a grim line. "Wednesdays are half days for me," he finally says. "I see patients in the morning, and spend the afternoon making notes. Sometimes I do that in the office, sometimes I do it here."

"So you came home?"

"Not right away. I went to lunch. Bixby's. I sat at the counter. Turkey on rye and coffee. Then I stopped at Lowe's. I needed weather stripping."

"The back door is drafty," his mother adds.

"I drove home after that, but it took a whole lot longer than usual."

"Black ice on the roads," Bistro recalls.

"Yes."

"Did you use your credit card at Lowe's?"

His father shakes his head. "Cash. But I have the receipt."

"We save all our receipts for the month in a folder," his mother says. "In the bottom drawer of our desk in the den."

"Good. You'll need it." Bistro turns back to Dad. "What time did you leave Lowe's?"

"That'll be on the receipt, won't it?"

Bistro nods. "It will, and we can stop now and get it, or you can give me an estimate and we can move through the rest of your afternoon."

"Three. Three fifteen," his father says.

"And you drove home from there?"

"That's correct."

"You told me you spent the afternoon in your office."

"I usually do."

"We questioned you the day after Lindsey disappeared," Bistro points out. "You forgot that fast?"

"My daughter was missing, Detective. At that point for an entire day. It *felt* like a week."

"Longer," Micah's mother whispers.

"It's my usual habit to stay in the office and make notes."

"So why didn't you on January twelfth?"

Micah's father sits back. He folds his arms over his chest. "Aren't you going to read me my rights?"

"Not yet," Bistro replies, and waits.

"I made a mistake," his father insists. "I don't always look at the clock. I wanted to fix the door," he says. "I picked up some caulking, too, and needed natural light to seal the window in the laundry room. I've been meaning to do it since, I don't know, last winter."

Bistro nods. He makes a note. "So you drove straight home from Lowe's? How long did that take you?"

His father shrugs and says, "An hour?"

"That long?" Bistro's eyebrows arch. "Oh, yeah," he says, "the black ice."

Micah's father nods. "A lot of cars were spinning out.

They were in ditches or stalled in the middle of the freeway."

"So the driving was slow."

"That's right. But you can check weather reports from that day. I bet it was all over the evening news."

Bistro nods. "We checked." He flips a page in his notebook. "Then what? You left Lowe's and headed for home? You didn't stop anywhere else?"

Micah notices the way his father's eyelid flickers, how his face is pulled into a tight frown. A long moment passes, into which Bistro says, "Your son has been honest with us, Dr. Hamilton. Maybe you could do the same."

Dad's stare almost sears him. "You spoke to Detective Bistro?"

Micah nods.

His father turns to Bistro. "I told you not to question him."

"I had your wife's permission. Who are you trying to protect, Dr. Hamilton? Micah or yourself?"

"You have no physical proof that ties either of us to Lindsey's death."

"Actually, we do." The tension in the room thickens so that Micah almost chokes on it. "We have preliminary results on your shoes, Dr. Hamilton."

His father's face pales.

"You were at the scene, sir," says Bistro. "Of that we're certain. So was Micah. We have a full cast of one hand. I think it'll be a perfect match to Micah's. He knelt beside your daughter. He probably picked her up and held her. There's enough evidence to suggest that. But what did *you* do, Dr. Hamilton? When were you there? Was it before Lindsey was killed? During? After? That's what we're trying to figure out."

Micah's mother falls back in her chair. She chokes through her next breath.

"After," his father whispers into the silence. "During." The word is jagged, hushed, but seems to peel back the top layer of Micah's skin.

"Kelley told you Lindsey was pregnant," Bistro continues.

"She called me, that afternoon. She was worried." His father snorts. "Worried about *herself*. She was livid, shrieking about 'lost opportunities'—all *she* had lost. She kicked Lindsey off the track team that morning. That was her reaction. She washed her hands of Lindsey. That fast. But it wasn't over."

That's why Lindsey wrote the note. She was kicked off the track team. January twelfth. And it's why Lindsey had on her uniform, Micah thinks. It makes sense. Kelley kicked her off the team, and Lindsey's response was in-your-face refusal.

"What time was that?"

His dad rubbed a hand over his face. "I was leaving Lowe's, so it was after three. She said she was looking for Lindsey. That someone needed to talk sense into her. Kelley wasn't ready to give up everything."

"Kelley had a lot to lose," Bistro agrees. "But you had more." He opens a folder. "You mortgaged this house, Mr. Hamilton, back in June of last year."

Micah's heart takes a nosedive. He knew they were hurting for money. That's the reason they sold his car. But he didn't know his parents would risk the house to make Lindsey's dream come true.

"We knew then that Lindsey had a chance. A real chance to make it. The path to the Olympics isn't cheap."

"It was the only way," his mother agrees.

"Everything costs money." His father ticks things off on his fingers. "Kelley wasn't cheap. Lindsey went through shoes by the month—that alone was two thousand dollars a year. Quality food, the competitions in Washington, Tennessee, and

New Jersey. And she had seven more between this season and next, just to qualify."

"You put a lot of money into Lindsey. A lot of time." His voice is steady, like the slow drip of water on stone. "A lot of pride."

"You mean, I was the father of a premier athlete? One of the best in the world? Yeah, I had that."

"And a lot of face to lose, Dr. Hamilton."

"I didn't raise a child who throws away opportunity."

"Was that part of it, too? Your parenting skills?" Bistro presses. "You couldn't stand the neighbors talking about a teenage pregnancy?"

"Questioning what kind of father I am," Micah's father says. "I'm a good dad—involved, but not overbearing. I'm concerned. I'm interested."

"We supported Lindsey," Mom says. "All of us."

"But it wasn't enough."

"I guess not," Dad says.

"That lit your fire, didn't it? It really burned you. You did so much for Lindsey, and she threw it all away."

His father's face seems to turn to stone. "Yes, I was angry," he admits.

"Enraged?" Bistro prompts.

But his father shakes his head. "That's not the way it happened. When I found Lindsey . . . By the time I got there"—his father's voice breaks—"I wasn't mad anymore. I was already thinking about what we could do to fix it. My mind had already gone through the possible scenarios. If Lindsey wanted to keep the baby, what we could do. If she didn't . . . what we could do."

"So what happened?"

"I saw her running through the orchard. Lindsey's coat

was bright red. Even through the trees I could see her move, so graceful, so much more a part of the wind than of her body and its limitations. She had that, you know? The ability to transcend her body's limitations. It was beautiful," he finishes.

"Who was with Lindsey?" Bistro asks.

His father tries to wave away the question. "I was in my car, and Lindsey cut north, away from the road and deeper into the orchard. Soon I couldn't even see her."

"But you got out of your car," Bistro leads.

"Yes."

"And you went into the orchard."

His father nods. "I did. But they had gone pretty far—"

"Who?" Bistro demands, "Lindsey and who else?"

"Micah. Micah was there. It was too late, but he wouldn't give up, even when Lindsey was lost to him."

And the memory unfolds in front of Micah's eyes. Lindsey running, lifted by the wind, and his trying to catch up. Glimpses of her as she weaves through the trees. And then their father, standing as solid as a plank, as unmoving, and Lindsey crumpled and curled at his feet.

"You killed her?" he breathes.

"No," Mom cries. "No."

"Lost how?" Bistro asks, trying to weave together the threads of the unraveling confession.

"Dead. Micah tried to pick her up. He wanted to carry her to the car. He was hysterical." His father looks at him and says, "You can't bring the dead back. No matter how sorry you are."

II

9:20 P.M.

Vivian arrived soon after Bistro left with Micah's father. They're sitting on the couch in the living room, not really watching a documentary on the History Channel, when his mother comes in and perches on the edge of the sofa. She clasps her hands between her knees.

"Vivian? Did Micah tell you how sorry I am about your mother?"

"Thank you, Mrs. Hamilton," Vivian replies.

"They arrested my husband today," his mother says. "The police. They came here tonight so sure it was Micah or my husband who killed Lindsey. The evidence, they said, could go either way."

Bistro had formally arrested his father. He called for backup, then cuffed his father and sat with him on the porch steps until the cruiser arrived. Micah and his mother watched from the living room. She stood as still as the air, except her hands—they fluttered in front of her like bird's wings. Micah's eyes were too dry to tear up. His heart beat so slowly, he had to wait for every breath.

"I know." Vivian wasn't surprised when Micah called. She

stayed on the phone with him until she pulled into the drive-way.

"He didn't do it, of course," Mom continues. "I know that."

Neither of them answer her. Vivian probably doesn't know what to say; Micah is pinned to the sofa, watching darkness roll toward him like a tornado.

He did it. His mom thinks so. And that's enough to make his world go to black.

"Do you want to know how I know?"

Vivian says, "Sure, Mrs. Hamilton."

"It will disappoint you, Vivian," she warns. "And surprise you, Micah."

His mother stands. She pulls a slip of paper from her pocket. "It's that receipt from Lowe's. Your father, he's never been good about time. But he's always been good about family." She flattens the receipt on her palm and uses her fingers to iron out the wrinkles. "He bought that caulking like he said. And the weather stripping, too. But he did it at four ten.

"Lindsey died between four fifteen and four forty-five. It's in the coroner's report.

"There was no time for him to find Lindsey. To argue with her . . ." Her voice trails into silence. "There was no time to get angry."

Micah feels himself separate from his body, like a split-ting atom. He implodes; the shredded pieces of his organs, of bone and cartilage, float, banking side to side, and pile up in his stomach. He might puke.

"There's only one reason your father would lie about it," his mother says. "We both know what that is."

And she stares at the receipt in her hand. She folds it and slides it back into her pocket. "I don't know what to do with it." The full weight of her gaze falls on Micah. "Damned if you do and damned if you don't."

He stares at his reflection in the bathroom mirror. The shower is running, but turned to cold, so that his face is clear, sharp, real.

The face of a murderer.

He's taken off his clothes, and his bare feet sink deeply into the throw rug. Sky blue. Lindsey's favorite color, but still boy enough that Micah agreed to have it in the bathroom they shared.

"I killed Lindsey," he says. He watches his lips move, barely revealing his teeth, creating only a ripple of movement across his face. "I'm a murderer."

His hand twitches and he almost drops the pocketknife.

His heart is beating. His lungs expand. He was so sure he'd lost both when his mother waved the receipt in front of him.

He thought for sure he was done when Vivian stood up, shakily, and told him, "I'm going home now." Nodding, backing away from him, shattering the bond that held them together. "I'm leaving," she repeated, then turned and ran out the door.

He's lost everything.

His peripheral vision crowds with the bold, carved faces of rock; with the dome of a gray sky etched with the bony fingers of trees, reaching toward him. They will pluck him out of this world and drop him into the next.

He's ready. He wants to go. There's peace in that world. There's Lindsey.

She turns and smiles at him. Her gold hair is flying around her head. She's running and loving it.

Lindsey is running races and winning them all. Micah wants that, even if all he gets to do is sit in the crowd and watch.

He runs the tips of his fingers over the veins in his wrist. Beneath them, he feels the beat of his heart. Oxygen. It pushes the blood through his body. But not anymore.

The knife has a thin, sharp blade, and Micah doesn't have to do much more than lay it against his skin before it draws blood. A little more pressure and the job is done. Burn and flow. Micah is reduced to his senses. First, feel and sight. He looks beyond his arm to his reflection in the bathroom mirror. His blood is cherry red and full of life. It curls its way down his arm, collects in the depression inside his elbow, and then pours onto the vanity.

This is dying.

The words knock around inside his head, elusive, and he really doesn't have the will to chase them.

I'm dying. Right now.

No, some part of his mind whimpers.

Denial. He's a master at it. For eleven days, he denied killing Lindsey. He believed in his innocence. Clung to it. He blocked out every shred of memory that would incriminate him. Denial. It's a sweet place to live. If there were a town called Denial, he'd move to it. He'd be an upstanding citizen.

Micah laughs. It sounds more like he's choking.

Truth is a bitch. It's got teeth. It tears into your flesh, jaws locked, a pit bull. Yeah, truth is a pit bull.

Micah stumbles backward. He drops his pocketknife, and it lands softly on the blue oval rug he's standing on.

Only it's not blue anymore, and he's not riding the clouds like he thought.

He sinks to the floor and his head falls back against the wall.

Blood. It's everywhere. Dripping from the edge of the vanity into a puddle on the tile floor; streaming down the oak cabinets in front of him; collecting on the rug.

His mom. She's going to have to clean it.

And bury him.

No. No.

Yes, she'll have to bury him, like she did Lindsey. And he remembers her that day, so light on her feet, the wind could have knocked her over. She's been that way ever since—more air than matter.

It's a family trait.

They're a flock of birds.

This time, when Micah laughs, it gurgles in his throat and pours out of him like the flow of blood.

I'm drowning.

He takes a swipe at his face: tears and mucus.

He looks at the cut in his wrist. It's a thin separation of skin. Such a small way to die. He watches his pulse. As it slows, so does the flow of blood.

His blood. And so much of it . . .

Micah hears his breath shudder. The sob tear through his chest.

He doesn't want to die.

"No. No, I don't."

But he can't live, either. He can't live and have Lindsey dead. He can't be the one who killed her.

He gasps through another round of tears. And this time

the smell of his blood fills his nose, so thick he gags on it.

This is death. My death.

And then fear catches up with him. Thins his breath. "I don't want to die."

But he can't take it back. None of it.

He cradles his arm, holds it against his chest.

Lindsey is gone, and now he is, too.

He rolls onto his side, draws his knees to his chest, and clutches his arm.

It's not too late. For either of them. It can't be.

He reaches for his T-shirt, crumpled on the floor beside him, but can't close his fingers over it. If he could lift it, wrap his arm, he could stop the blood. He could stop the dying. He has to.

But he couldn't for Lindsey . . .

An image explodes in his mind. It's Lindsey's face again. Tears streaming from her eyes. And this time, the movie comes with sound.

"My life is over, Micah," she says.

"It's not," he insists.

"I've ruined everything."

"Why? What happened?"

She chokes on a sob. "I fell in love. Stupid, huh?"

"With Reed?"

"Jonas. Try to keep up, brother."

"Jonas? He was last year."

She laughs, only it sounds like a whining saw. "Tell that to our baby."

Micah, body and soul, goes into deep freeze.

"Yeah. Stupid. So it's over for me," she continues. "It can't get any more over than that."

"Yeah," he agrees. "Totally."

"Thanks," Lindsey says. "That's helping."

He tries to shake off the shock and look for a better outcome. But his sister is right. "It's over."

"Shut up," she says.

"London," he mutters. "The Olympics. Gold medal." Her losses are slipping through his mind, through his lips. "Four-seventeen."

"Shut up!" Lindsey screams. "Just shut up." She shoves him backward. "It's not like you're going anywhere, Micah. It's not like you're MLB. Who's going to take on a cheater?" She was losing it, tears and mucus and words spilling from her in a great rush. "No college. No team. No girlfriend."

Lindsey pushes past him, back onto the track, her long hair snapping in the wind. He watches that, the ends of her hair, as she streaks down the inside lane, and then time and scenery shift and Micah is running now, too, surrounded by the columns of apple trees on Bryce's Farm.

"Faster!" Lindsey's desperate voice calls, and she throws a glance over her shoulder. "She's coming, Micah!"

He knows it. He feels her behind him.

Kelley had passed them in town. She stopped her car and rolled down the window. "The two losers," she jeered. "The Hamilton has-beens." Her smile was a shark's.

"My life isn't over," Lindsey had said. "I have years of running ahead of me." But you don't.

"Don't kid yourself," Kelley retorted. "You're finished."

"You lost, and you just keep on losing," Lindsey said, then she grabbed Micah's arm and they raced across the street, toward the state road, toward Bryce's Farm, toward home.

Kelley followed, tore past them on the street, so close Micah's fingers glanced off the side of her car. He remembers the sting, the choking certainty that Kelley meant to harm them.

Then she stopped, climbed out of the car, and chased them into the trees.

There's no cover in the orchard. Winter stripped and tossed the leaves to the ground. And it's too late for him, anyway. He hears her breath, feels it on his neck. Micah is no competition for Kelley. Years after Athens, she's still faster than the average athlete. But she doesn't want him. She darts around him, and the branches snap back and hit him in the face. They draw blood that blurs his vision, but Micah keeps running.

Lindsey's red coat gives her away. It's the only color in the gray day. She weaves through the trees, but Kelley anticipates her and goes straight. They collide, and Kelley pounces. She looks so much like a big cat that for a moment it's almost as if he were watching a cougar. Then her hands are on Lindsey's neck, leather gloves stretched taut against her knuckles. Her momentum knocks them to the ground.

And Lindsey's head, that soft spot above her ear, cracks against the sharp edge of a stone and opens. Blood, a bright red stream of it, runs into her hair, curls around her neck, drips onto the frozen earth.

Micah doesn't know he's stopped running until Kelley stands up, Lindsey's necklace tangled in her fingers. White plumes of breath sear the air in front of Kelley. She's pale, frozen, statuesque. Except her eyes. Dark. Flared. Fear. Felony.

"Oh, God." Micah breaks the silence, and Kelley stirs. Her head swivels toward him. She's stunned, but waking from it; her rage is thawing.

"Micah!" She gasps his name, like his presence is a surprise, like all that just transpired is news to her.

He falls to his knees beside Lindsey. He turns her face in his hands, looks into her eyes.

Reflection, but no life.

"Gone. She's. Gone."

He hears his voice, shattered so much that each syllable is its own sentence.

He turns to Kelley. "Help me," he begs. "Help Lindsey."

But Kelley backs away, stumbling. She turns and runs. And Lindsey's necklace, the silver chain with the charm of Mercury's foot, still tangled in Kelley's hand, shimmers in the weak rays of the sun.

The memory—or the blood loss—makes Micah lose consciousness. He passes out as the image of Lindsey's necklace weaves and sparkles in the last stream of sunlight of January twelfth. He doesn't know how long he's out, but it's Vivian's voice that saves him. Vivian and his mother.

Crying, both of them. His mother's keening, really, sounding more animal than human. Vivian grabs a hand towel and wraps it around his wrist. She tells his mother to call 911.

"Micah," Vivian calls to him. "Micah Robert Hamilton, you wake up. *Right now.*" Like all he's done is fallen into a nap. "You wake up and listen to what I have to say. Your mother is wrong. She is."

He feels the towel tighten on his arm and then pressure. His eyes flick open, and he sees Vivian kneeling over him, putting all her strength into her hands, binding his wrist.

She stares into his eyes. "I *know* it," she says. "I know *you.*"

"I remember," he manages, his voice a thinning thread.

"Well, you remember wrong," Vivian says, willing him her strength, her conviction of his innocence. "You didn't kill Lindsey. There's no room in your heart for it."

"You're an authority on that?"

"On Micah Hamilton, I am," she insists. Her voice is pure confidence.

He lifts his free hand and brushes her cheek. "Thanks," he says. "But I know." And he lets the weight of his words settle on her. "I didn't kill Lindsey, because Kelley did."

"You remember that?"

He nods, weakly. "Yes, I remember. I remember it all now."

His mother is back, holding the cordless phone to her ear. She sinks to the floor, crying.

"I'm sorry. Sorry," she says.

"I know, Mom."

But she's rocking, crying, beyond reaching.

Micah fades in and out, always waking to his mother's crying, and to Vivian's steady presence, her reassuring words.

"You're going to be okay," she says.

"I am," he agrees. "Now."

Even if no one else believes him, he knows. For sure. Beyond any doubt. He didn't kill Lindsey. But he has to try to set them straight. Everyone. For his sister. And for his father.

"Call Bistro," he tells Vivian. "Tell him it was Kelley. Tell him she has Lindsey's necklace. That she tore it off Lindsey's throat when she was choking her."

"I'll call him. But you're the one who's going to tell him."

Her determination makes him smile. He rests, feels the feathery pulse in his throat, then says, "You didn't really know."

"I knew. I've always known." Her cheeks flush. "Well, except for about sixty seconds," she admits. "But it was all so much. Your mom on the edge like that. You slipping away. I'm sorry I ran out on you."

"I'm surprised you came back."

"I didn't even get a mile down the road," she says, and smiles. "That's when I heard your voice inside my head. What you said to your dad, that you never hurt anyone. Ever. It's true.

"Bistro's simmering-pot theory never applied to you; that's why he arrested your dad. Because he couldn't find anyone who could say they ever saw you angry."

That's true. He takes a loss as hard as anyone during the season, but he never loses his cool. Not on the mound, and not off it.

He settles back inside himself, into renewed strength, a confidence that hasn't been there for a while. Vivian talks to him nonstop. Mostly about what they'll be doing together: her dance at Viet school, driving up to Seattle for a Mariners game, their senior year. Eventually, the high wail of a siren breaks through, followed by a commotion that's all sharp angles and edges. The paramedics arrive, are fast and abrupt, and carry him away.

Epilogue

MARCH 2012

Micah did pick up Lindsey. He held her, looked into her eyes, and saw himself. There was no life in her. He placed his cheek against her nose, and the absence of breath was unacceptable. Micah remembers it all now. That was when he began to lose the feel of reality, when his body became more liquid than matter. He put his mind into a mental shredder. He ran as far away from the truth as he could.

Kelley killed his sister.

That night, she drove all the way to Tacoma and ditched her size seven-and-a-half Nike Air Max shoes in a Dumpster behind a Target. She tucked Lindsey's necklace into a blue velvet jewelry case and stuffed that in the corner of a drawer in her dresser.

She couldn't bear to part with it, she said, because it was all she had left of Lindsey.

Kelley got her chance to speak after her trial. She stood up at sentencing and said, "I loved Lindsey. Everything about her. I never meant to kill her. I just lost it, you know?"

And Micah does know, because he was there. But he will never understand that kind of rage. How it can snap a person in two.

He read her confession. Bistro gave him a copy, and Micah is keeping it.

Remembering was the hardest thing he's ever had to do. It was losing Lindsey twice. Micah's therapist is right about that. And continuing to remember her loss is healthy, she says, so long as he doesn't dwell on it. So long as he talks about it, because when he does, its grip on him loosens.

"Micah?" his mother calls from the bottom of the stairs.

She's doing better now, too. They all are. It was eating her up inside, that she thought Micah killed Lindsey. That she believed it, if only for a few minutes.

There was a time when he believed that his father could have killed Lindsey; and when his father thought the same about him.

He gets it now, how extreme emotions can twist perspective.

He doesn't blame his parents. Loss as deep as Lindsey's is a long road to travel, like his grandfather talked about. They're doing a good job of navigating their way now.

He can't say the same for Reed. He's slowly fading away. He's not on the team this year, and most days Micah doesn't even see him at school. And right now, Micah's okay with that.

He hears the crunch of gravel from the driveway below. The soft purr of the Mini's engine. Viv is here, but he's not ready. There's one more thing he needs to do.

Micah stands on the threshold of what was Lindsey's bedroom—they turned it into a den. A family room. The walls are a living scrapbook that celebrates their lives. There are some pictures of Lindsey; her medals; a pair of sneakers they got bronzed; and now her necklace, Mercury's foot dangling from the silver chain. Bistro brought it back to them today, and Micah wants it where he can see it. Linds never took that necklace off. It reminded her of possibility. And now it does the same for Micah.

There are pictures of Micah in uniform; a ball in a plastic case that was his five hundredth strikeout; his first baseball glove, passed down from his grandfather. There are pictures of Dad on his high school track team—they got in touch with Jefferson High, his alma mater, which was happy to help. The school even sent an old jersey. His father had to wrestle himself into it, and it fit like skin, but he was happy to have it.

His mother hadn't played formal sports in high school. They dug through a box of old photos, and Micah's grandfather sent a few of his favorites, too: teenaged Mom, riding a horse and wearing a straw cowboy hat; standing astride a bicycle on a trail crowded with full, green trees; at age ten with a bat against her shoulder and her arm around the waist of her older brother.

The bed is gone, the dresser, and all of Lindsey's clothes and possessions, too. Now there are chairs, a coffee table, and bookshelves. Sometimes Micah does his homework in here. Sometimes he finds his mom or dad in here reading.

"Micah!" his mother calls again. "Vivian's here. We're going to be late."

Late to the first game of the season.

Bistro didn't tell the school about how Micah bought his chem grade, but Micah did. He sat out last year and his dream took a big hit—USC doesn't want him, but that's all right. He wouldn't want to be there without Lindsey, anyway. He didn't rat on the kid who helped him, and that didn't score him any points with the school or the Commission. He can live with that. What he did was wrong, and no one else needs to pay for his mistake.

He's not completely washed up, though. MLB isn't out of reach, but it'll take more discipline, more determination to get there—and he has that.

His arm is better than ever. He and Dad put a lot of time in together at the cages, and in the backyard, where Micah worked his arm while his mom and Vivian played cheer-leaders. That was when he missed Lindsey most, because she would have been there with them—cheering him on—for sure.

"Coming!"

He tucks his mitt under his arm and closes the door, then changes his mind and swings it open. It's getting easier, liv-ing with only the memory of Lindsey.

Suzanne Marie Phillips is the author of the critically acclaimed *Chloe Doe* and *Burn*. *Lindsey Lost* is her first suspense novel—and she loved writing it so much that she's working on another.

She lives with her family in California and Oregon.